THE
ATLANTIAN
CHRONICLES

ATLANTIS RISING

GARY ENGLISH

outskirtspress
DENVER, COLORADO

The Atlantian Chronicles
Atlantis Rising
All Rights Reserved.
Copyright © 2014 Gary English
v2.0

Outskirts Press, Inc.
http://www.outskirtspress.com

Paperback ISBN: 978-1-4787-0147-7
Hardback ISBN: 978-1-4787-2313-4

Outskirts Press and the "OP" logo are trademarks belonging to Outskirts Press, Inc.

PRINTED IN THE UNITED STATES OF AMERICA

To friends and family who supported and encouraged me along the way, and whose suggestions I found invaluable.
Thanks.

INTRODUCTION

Have you ever thought about people such as you and me living on Atlantis? I did, at the young age of thirteen. My youthful mind thrived on reading mythology and science fiction. One day I discovered an entry that Plato had written about Atlantis, and came to believe that it actually existed. I often mused about what may have happened to this city, wondered *what if* anyone had survived, and considered how it could happen. Thus the kernel of the idea behind this story was planted. As I grew older, science became my passion, learning about *why* and *how* things actually worked. I indulged my curiosity and studied chemistry, physics, geology and zoology, with a smattering of astronomy on the side. Science fiction movies such as *Forbidden Planet, Flash Gordon,* and *The Time Machine* fed my appetite for answers to the unknown.

More time passed, I grew up, took on the responsibilities of supporting a family, and joined the Navy. For over ten years I served our country on both a submarine and destroyer, eventually taking an instructor's position in the Mideast. It was there, alone and lost in my thoughts with little to do, that I purchased my first *IBM compatible* computer (a reverse engineered version of the original PC), and started to compose my first novel, *Atlantis Rising.*

From the imagination of that thirteen-year-old boy evolved this tale which attempts to answer all the *what if* questions I once held, and possibly some of those you've had as well. It is my sincere expectation that, after you read the first of these chronicles, you will be eager to read my next installment and enjoy the journey into the world I've envisioned possible.

CHAPTER ONE

"*Freedom-Nine* to *Skyoil-One,* approaching your location ETA about fifteen minutes request helipad illumination."

"*Skyoil-One* Roger that, helipad is illuminated, waiting your approach. What is the nature of your arrival?"

"Two execs here for inspection," came the pilot's reply.

"They weren't expected until Tuesday," commented the operator.

"Yeah, I know," came the pilot's reply, "but what are you going to do when the higher-ups get a hair up their ass? I say, just go with the flow and collect your paycheck."

Corey chuckled. "Yeah, I know that for sure. See you in fifteen, *Skyoil-One* out." Calling out over his shoulder to the first person he saw, he instructed, "Tell Mr. Holbrook the execs he was expecting Tuesday will be here in fifteen minutes."

Dashing out of the control center, Jenkins mumbled, "Oh brother, Dave ain't gonna like this."

The oil rig was impressive from the air. Visible only as a spot on the horizon less than an hour ago, it now sprawled below the helicopter like a metal island. Staring down at the expanse of antennas, tanks, and booms, Tom couldn't shake the image of the rig as being the tallest skyscraper amid a flooded city. From this vantage point the sea appeared the texture of carpet, being one of those rare calm days on the open Atlantic. The setting sun provided an excellent indirect light; the entire scene appeared bas-relief. The small breakers accentuated the size of the construction, making its two hundred plus feet appear all the more imposing.

Just before the copter landed, Tom reached over to Bob, shaking him in order to rouse him from his stupor. Stepping onto the helo pad a small, quick fellow immediately introduced himself as David Holbrook. "I hope you had a decent flight. You picked a good day to make the trip—it's been a while since we had it this easy out here. Let's just drop off your luggage, and I'll give you the cook's tour before supper."

Upon unloading their suitcases in the staterooms, David rapidly showed them every room of the microcosmic city in an hour and a half of nonstop motion, narrating it with a fast, enthusiastic monologue. The only real information Tom was able to hang onto was that David was the chief engineer of the site, and had been aboard for the past year or so. He became convinced that he would be carrying the map of the rig David provided for the rest of his life—the thing was quite a bit bigger than the previous rig he'd visited, and there was virtually no resemblance in the layout.

By the time the three of them had made their way to the control center on the upper level, Tom was breathing hard and Bob was nearly sober. Tom glanced around the room, recognizing most, but not all, of the intricate production and flow regulation equipment. One entire section was new to him. "What's that?" he asked David.

"As you know we have all the standard petroleum-handling safety features, and all the normal damage control measures as well. That section there is pretty much a measure of last resort—it's the activation controller for the SSBOP, self-sealing blowout pressure system, basically an explosive seal. Heard of it?"

Tom nodded. "I'm acquainted with the theory, but I've never actually dealt with one."

"Pretty simple actually—this is the internal pressure monitor subsection, that is the external one. We set the thresholds here. If the parameters are exceeded, the fourteen shape charges at the base of the line go off simultaneously, closing the access to the well completely. You can also override and activate it manually over here," pointing to a panel to the left. "Of course if that happens we have to start drilling all over again after the crisis is over."

"Is it effective?"

David shrugged. "Don't know—on paper, yes, but it's never been used. We had to have it, though—an oil spill of any kind is bad news, but with the pressure we get from this access, it'd be a real disaster if we ruptured a main line. We can't afford a repeat of that Gulf oil spill catastrophe. Well, that'll do for now. It's about a half-hour until supper, so you two probably want to get started unpacking."

Tom nodded. Bob straightened up, muttering, "Unpack. Shower...." and headed out of the room. Tom followed right behind.

As he was getting to the bottom of his suitcase Tom heard the shower start in Bob's room. He smiled faintly, hoping his 'executive advisor' sobered up by dinnertime. He couldn't believe how much alcohol he drank on the flight from Chicago.

While choosing a shirt to wear to supper Tom paused to listen, becoming aware of a low, steady rumble. What was that? Not knowing if it had just begun, or he had just become aware of it, he listened more intently. The rumble grew louder. Tom heard Bob turn off the shower. There was a moment of silence from the next room, then Bob's voice called out.

"What the..." The rig heaved abruptly sideways slamming Bob to the floor, just as the lights went out.

The emergency lights cut in by the time Tom managed to get to his feet. Cautiously, he moved to the door, the floor beneath his feet still trembling slightly. Aftershocks. Tom opened the door into the passageway.

Dodging two running figures that burst from around the corner, Tom made his way to Bob's stateroom. Just as he arrived, Bob's door flew open and he darted into the hall, buttoning his shirt as he ran. Spotting Tom, he rushed to his side, narrowly avoiding another sprinting technician as he moved.

"What the hell..." yelled Tom.

Shoving a finger into Tom's face, Bob cut him off. "I don't know!

Let's get to control!" Bob turned and ran down the passageway with Tom following a few steps behind.

The room was in turmoil. David Holbrook was there, directing efforts to ascertain and control the damage. "Jenkins—status topside!"

"Pretty bad, we lost the helo over the side, two antennas out of commission, and a possible rupture in Storage Two. Mainline pressure is still normal, and most of primary piping seems to still be intact."

"Thank heaven for small favors! Corey—how are the electronics?"

A red-headed man seated at the console adjusted his glasses and looked up. "We took some damage in main metering, but the backup systems are functioning fine. Communications all operational using the antennas we still got."

"Check distress signal."

"Transmitting."

"Good, any replies?"

Corey shook his head. "Not yet. We're on all bands though—it shouldn't be much longer."

Turning his attention to the plotter's corner, Dave inquired, "What's the traffic report, Zack?"

The older man responded without looking up from his chart. "Only one vessel within hailing distance, a U.S. Naval ship about four hundred miles to the southeast. No other traffic in the area."

Turning back to Corey, the communications technician, David asked, "Any reply yet?"

"Just now—it's the Navy ship! They were heading south when they caught our hail and they've altered course this way; ETA just over twelve hours."

"Okay, good. Keep them on the line, and make sure they relay our report to any other vessels they can reach." Crossing the room to the primary display screen, David asked the technician monitoring it, "How's our situation below?" Bob and Tom caught up just as the young man replied.

"Two of the launches broke free, but the third is still moored and intact. There was no damage to the tanker in berth one, but two of its mooring lines snapped. They're being replaced as we speak." The tech glanced at the computer screen before him. "No trace of the helicopter. We've lost it completely."

Bob frowned. Without the helo, their link to land was severed. The small launches used for strut work and diver ops wouldn't take them a third of the way to the nearest solid ground.

Tom looked back and forth from David to Bob in anticipation. He wasn't aware of all the implications of the damage report, but he knew enough to know that they were in some serious trouble, and decided his wisest course of action would be to keep his mouth shut and pay attention.

Shouting from across the room, Corey reported, "I have Land Base on channel one, the Navy ship on two. Who do you want to talk to first?"

The three execs rushed over. Taking the microphone from Corey, David instructed, "Give me Land Base. Might as well clue them in with what little we know." A click of the mike, and he began. "Holbrook here, we have initial damage reports, and control measures are in progress. We've lost our helo and two launches. No personnel injuries reported, and all hands accounted for. There's no sign yet of what caused the whole thing. By some miracle, the main access wasn't damaged, and our major pressures have all been maintained. There was some damage topside. We're still assessing it. There's a U.S. Navy ship about twelve hours away. We're in communication with them on two right now. That's it for the moment, over."

"Read you. Keep a carrier wave on one, and update us every chance you get. We're on the line with seismology and oceanography, trying to find the disturbance. Nothing yet—it just came out of the blue. One minute we had a clear map, the next it's a Christmas tree. We'll inform you as soon as we get anything."

"Check, thanks." David turned to Corey. "Okay, go ahead and give me the ship."

Corey flipped some switches and signaled. Holbrook keyed the mike, "Testing."

A voice came over the receiver's speaker, "Reading you loud and clear. This is the Commander of the *USS Lavan*. We picked up your mayday. What is the extent of your damage?"

David keyed the mike. "The damage to the rig is extensive, but not irreparable. We have lost our helicopter and two of our three launches, and we are presently cut off from shore except for radio contact."

"Aye—we copy. Any injured personnel?"

"Negative—no one seriously hurt. Do you have any indication of what hit us?"

"None. We're not equipped for extensive oceanographic research, and none of our lookouts have spotted anything. Sonar did pick up a loud explosion on approximately your bearing, but we have no information about the source."

Thanking the commander, he handed the mike back to Corey. David turned to the two men he'd barely acknowledged. Seeing their bewildered expressions, he looked around the room and raised an eyebrow. "It looks like we've got a handle on the situation now. One of the things I'm worried about is that we really don't know what the situation is—I have no idea what hit us. There was a damn big wave, but I've seen bigger. Near as we can tell from our recorders, there were some ungodly high amplitude sub-surface shock waves. Worst I've ever seen."

Before David could utter another word, Bob blurted out, "What the hell did you just say?"

David smirked and reiterated, "We had an earthquake."

"What caused it?" Tom queried.

"That's the million dollar question about now. You heard them—nobody has even a good guess. That includes us. We've had the standard monitoring of the bottom going on for over a year now, and there were none of the normal precursors to anything of this magnitude. Whatever it was—volcano, fissure opening, whatever—it was very big and very sudden."

Motioning them to the main plotting board, David spread out a chart showing the bottom contours for a fifty-nautical mile radius, centered on the oil rig. There were no extremely deep trenches or sudden depth changes. The bottom of this area was gently sloping without any irregularities. The two men drew closer to the table for a better look.

"The best estimate of direction for the original disturbance was about here," announced David, pointing at a spot generally south of the rig. "Of course, not knowing what the origin was, we can't find out how far away it began."

"Is the Navy ship the only recent traffic you've had?" asked Tom, eyeing the print suspiciously.

David nodded. "The surface search radar hasn't had another contact for three or four days. The antenna was totaled by the shock, so it's not operating now. Still, unless something's moving real fast, it's not going to cover the hundred clear miles we had at last look any time soon."

Tom was still studying the chart with intent. "There aren't any active volcanoes charted in that area."

"That's right. That was one of the beauties of locating here. As this part of the Atlantic goes, it's very stable, geologically. There's not even a decent-sized sea mount for almost fifteen miles, and that one's not going to hurt anyone."

Bob frowned. "So what made the big noise?"

David shrugged. He looked once more at the chart. "I sure wish I knew."

"Maybe it wasn't natural," Tom said. Both men looked at him.

"Well, you've got to admit that there should have been some warning if this were a geological phenomenon," he began a little defensively.

"So what's your point? What else could make a mess this size?" Bob asked, puzzled by Tom's suggestion.

"What do you know about nuclear testing?"

Bob caught himself just before he scoffed at the idea. *Surely the Navy would have given us some warning*, he thought. After a moment he amended that assumption. Only the U.S. Navy would at least alert them—*wouldn't they?*

David also seemed to be taking the idea half seriously. A cataclysm of this size had to be brought about by something other than standard explosions, and a nuclear test would certainly fit the bill.

The three stood silent, lost in thought in the midst of the busy room. Recovery efforts were well under way, and most of the damage would be repaired in the course of the next few days. None of that would matter, however, if they were hit again.

Tom shook his head while thinking, *It might be harder next time.* The thought filled him with foreboding. He opened his mouth to ask David about their chances of surviving a similar occurrence, but before he could speak there was a cry of alarm from across the room.

David rushed over, Bob and Tom a step behind. The operator who yelled was staring up at one of the four video monitors over his console, his jaw slack. Following his gaze they looked up at the screen. The display had been following recovery efforts on the first external level, forty feet above the waterline on the south side. The camera had panned around, momentarily pointing out at the ocean. The water was illuminated for many yards around the metal island by the flood lights topside. Just beyond the wash of light over the waves, however, something was happening. The actual surface of the sea was not being reflected from the rig's lighting, but by something just under the surface. The technician froze the camera on that spot.

The monitor's resolution wasn't optimum for sightings at the apparent range of the glow, but all the men sensed something unusual in that light. With the exception of Tom, they were all acquainted with normal ocean phosphorescence and the various light-emitting sea life. This light didn't resemble anything so familiar. For one thing, it was a little too bluish. The color of the glow was decidedly unnatural in appearance. It also seemed to have a definite shape, although its form was not easily discernible over the monitor screen. The entire control center's activity stopped as people gathered around the monitor.

Breaking the momentary silence, David directed the transfixed operator at the controls, "Get one and three on that, and get that recorder going. This might be worth keeping track of." As the technician hurried to obey, David spoke to a large black man who had entered the room. "Paul, what's going on up there?"

"Repairs in progress. We should be able to take care of most of it right here."

"No, I don't mean that. I mean that!" He pointed to the screen.

Looking at the screen, Paul scowled as his eyes caught the vague shape of the glow, and stated, "What the hell's that?" Without waiting for an answer, he turned and ran out of the room. Tom considered following him, but couldn't take his eyes off the display.

As the crew watched, the unknown light become brighter and brighter, taking on clearer form with each passing minute. It slowly became obvious that it was some sort of object rising closer to the surface. It was also approaching the oil rig at a slow but steady speed.

Tom finally got the resolve to tear his eyes from the monitor. He waved his hand in front of Bob who was mesmerized, as was everyone in the room. Once he had his attention, he pointed to himself, then upward.

Bob paused only a second before nodding eagerly and making his way through the crowd around him to the door. With Tom on his heels, he left the control center and began navigating the maze of corridors and ladders heading out to the first level.

Following almost at a run, Tom spoke to Bob's back. "What's going on?"

Without looking back, Bob shrugged. "Hell, I don't know. The whole past hour's been a damn mystery to me. The shock wave bit itself was pretty scary, but God knows what we're about to see."

Upon reaching the door that led out to the deck, Bob paused a moment to catch his breath before opening the hatch. Tom came up a few steps behind him, panting but eager. Together they went outside.

The scene had changed considerably in the intervening minutes they'd been moving through the rig. The glow they had seen on the display was now less than a hundred yards away, and its form was fairly clear. It seemed to be about forty feet in diameter. As they walked quickly to the rail, it became apparent that the object was heading for the surface. It had slowed its forward progress, so that it was barely moving toward them, but even as they watched it began to break the surface.

At first it appeared as a smooth, blue bubble. Tom's first impression of the object as translucent with an internal source of light was, upon closer inspection, incorrect. It appeared that the bubble was made of an opaque substance which itself glowed with that odd luminescence.

The bubble increased in size, while slowly broaching the surface. It seemed about half-exposed when the hatch behind Tom burst open and most of the group which had been in the control center ran out to the rail. Three of the men had weapons, two were carrying rifles, and Greg had a 12-gauge shotgun. He was carrying a bag of shells, and loaded the gun as he came toward the rail.

Noticing Tom's look, he shrugged and said, "Just in case."

The men returned their attention to the glowing object, now almost completely exposed. It was, Tom noticed, not a totally smooth surface. It seemed unbroken around the entire visible perimeter, but the hemispherical skin was mottled, giving it an appearance not unlike a view of the moon. He became conscious of the sounds around him: sounds of equipment clattering, some incredulous comments by the watching crowd of a dozen or so, and the ever present low rumble of the sea. Then he noticed something strange—he didn't hear anything unusual.

The blue bubble, though now only twenty or thirty yards away, didn't seem to be making a sound. There were some noises from the small waves hitting its sides, but no sound was emanating from the object itself. It struck both Bob and Tom that it was very odd that something this size could be so quiet. Both were examining the base of the bubble for some evidence of propulsion or flotation devices. They found none.

Footsteps sounded behind them, as two more men came to the rail to observe. Bob noted mentally that this left only five men in the control center. It was more than enough to operate the necessary systems, but he couldn't help but wonder if it would be wiser to have another body or two handy in case another emergency arose. He didn't have time to take any action, however…the bubble opened.

It wasn't a break so much as it was a clean part in the surface. A curved triangle in the side toward the rig apparently slid aside. Wide at the bottom, narrowing to a point at the top center of the bubble, the appearance was as if someone had cut out a sixth of a dome-shaped cake.

The man to Bob's left leaned on the rail and aimed the rifle he was carrying at the opening in the bubble. At the sound of the hammer being cocked, Bob quickly turned. "What the hell are you doing?"

The crewman's eyes didn't move from the bubble, he simply stated, "Ready for anything."

"You mean, 'ready to shoot anything'?"

"Only if I need to." The marksman's attention didn't waver.

Bob slowly turned his eyes back to the opening in the blue object. He didn't have to wait long. As he watched, three men appeared in the opening. In the light provided by the spotlights trained on the dome by the rig, he could make out the men quite clearly. They all seemed relatively young, early thirties, Bob guessed. They appeared to be pretty normal fellows; perhaps a little taller and paler than most, but overall just regular people.

Their craft had stopped completely now and was ten yards or so from the tower. The men looked up at the crowd and called out, their voices carrying remarkably well across the water, "Hello! You speak English, correct?"

Bob and Tom looked at each other. The speaker's language was quite clear, and neither man noticed a trace of an accent in his speech. His voice was a little higher and reedier than expected, but was otherwise unremarkable.

Paul, the big black topside coordinator, was the first to reply. "Who are you?" he yelled down at the men.

The same man replied, "I am Raval. You all speak English, correct?"

Tom found his voice. He leaned over the rail. "Yes, that's correct. We all speak English."

The three men nodded. The man who had been doing the talking, and who Tom assumed to be the nominal leader of the group, paused a moment and spoke again. "Please put away your weapons. It is not in our best interests to have them aimed at us."

"I don't think so," remarked the man next to Bob with a snort, while leveling his rifle. Sighting along the barrel, he made no move to rid himself of the gun. Bob glanced at him, and then looked back at the bubble.

One of the two silent men was looking in his direction. He seemed to be staring at the men along the rail, perhaps waiting. After a moment, he inclined his head slightly.

The man with the rifle on Bob's left snorted again, uncocked his weapon, and lowered it. Without saying a word, he straightened and tossed the gun over the rail into the dark water just below the platform. Bob looked startled and turned to the man, but his question was cut short by another announcement by the man in the bubble.

"We do not wish conflict. We do not desire to have combat with you." Raval stopped speaking for a moment and turned to the man on his right. After a time, he returned his attention to the men on the rail. "You will please now come aboard our vessel."

"Hell no!" exclaimed Paul, extending his middle finger. Bob and Tom looked at each other, perplexed. They sensed the growing unrest in the men.

"Do not be apprehensive, and please do not resist. The other five men aboard your construction will suffice to operate it. We simply wish to take you to our city."

"The nearest city's awful far away!" shouted the man who had tossed his rifle.

Raval half-smiled at him. "That's not exactly true anymore. We will travel no more than fourteen miles in this craft as you measure distance."

This last announcement brought about more consternation aboard the rig than the three men in the bubble had anticipated. The workers began to stir restlessly, eyeing the blue vessel and its occupants with suspicion. It was obvious to Tom that no one intended to get aboard that strange-looking craft.

The men aboard the blue bubble apparently realized this too. After appearing to confer with each other for a moment, Raval addressed the group again. "We insist that you join us aboard. We do not wish to be required to use force, but will do so if it is necessary."

An abrupt silence on the rig greeted this remark. The crewmen were momentarily startled into inaction. As they stood considering the threat, Raval spoke again.

"Observe," he said simply, turning his head slightly so that his gaze was directed at one of the two remaining large antennas mounted just above deck level on the oil rig. With no apparent further action on his part, the larger of the masts began melting at its center with alarming speed. It didn't change color, or give any normal sign of heating up. It simply became liquid for about a foot of its thirty foot length, and then the ten-inch diameter pole toppled onto the deck.

In the control room there was no way of determining what was being said, but it was obvious that the three strangers were speaking to and being answered by the crewmen topside.

"At least they speak English," David observed when he found his voice. There was no response from any of the remaining personnel, for they were transfixed by what they were witnessing.

After a few minutes of watching this silent conversation between the two parties, David saw one of the three encroachers tilt his head in the direction of part of the rig and make another speech. For a moment nothing happened, then he saw movement out of the corner of his eye, and glanced at the second monitor just in time to see the radio mast collapse.

"Holy shit!" he exclaimed, his eyes widening. At that instant the thinking part of his brain came back to life, his only thought being the welfare of the metal outpost. Quickly grabbing the young technician seated at the communication console, David shouted, "Reactivate the distress beacon! Get me the *Lavan* again! Get me Shore Base! Now! Now! Now! Now!" Looking feverishly back at the monitors, David's eyes were no longer drawn to the center one. His glance darted between the four screens, watching for further signs of destruction.

"Shit!" Paul cried, watching the already extensive damage to his precious exterior become even worse. He whirled on the waiting men on the blue bubble. "What the hell are you doing, you bastards?"

Raval was unshaken. "That was simply a demonstration. We do not desire to harm personnel or damage more of your equipment, but we will do so to the degree required to obtain your cooperation."

The group aboard the rig nervously exchanged glances. Bob was the first to speak up. "I think we'd better do what they want. The Navy ship isn't due for some time yet, and these clowns could destroy this whole platform by then. I have no idea where they plan to take us or what they want to do, but it's pretty obvious that if they just wanted to hurt us they could have done it by now." He looked at Tom.

Tom glanced around at the group. "He's right, guys. Maybe these people just want hostages or something, but apparently they don't simply want to kill people. I say we take them at their word and see what they have in store."

With resignation, most of the crew nodded. A couple of their faces showed raw fear, but most were simply nervous, as could be expected. Tom made a mental note to keep an eye on the ones who seemed the most scared. They might do something irrational and land the bunch of them in trouble.

Paul, moving slowly and cautiously, went to the side and lowered the ladder used to load the launchers. As he let the metal steps down, the strange blue craft approached until it was directly below them. One at a time, led by Bob and Tom, the fourteen men descended the ladder onto the deck of the bubble.

Tom was surprised the moment he stepped onto the surface of the vessel. It had more give than anything he'd ever been on. The feeling he got stepping on the unusual deck formed a mental image of stepping on the back of a whale.

When he looked over at Bob, he saw that the senior advisor had noticed the resilience as well. While waiting for the rest of the men to descend the ladder, the two of them looked closely at the surface and noticed that the floor glowed with the same light as the outer surface of the bubble. Bob leaned over to Tom and spoke softly, "Whole thing's probably made of the same stuff."

Tom nodded. "Ever seen anything like it?"

Bob raised his eyebrows and shook his head. "Nope, not that you could build anything out of anyway."

"Same here."

As soon as all the crewmen made it to the deck of the craft, it began to move away from the oil rig. At first almost imperceptibly, then with increasing speed, it headed south. When it was about a quarter mile away from the metal island, Raval and the other two walked toward the center of the bubble, motioning for the rest to follow them. Tom turned and gave the receding oil rig a last look. He wondered if it would be the last time he'd ever see it. It also occurred to him to wonder what the men left aboard thought about the events of the last fifteen minutes.

If it was him, he'd be damn curious. He turned and walked into the blue dome.

The communication operator looked up and held out a mike. "The *Lavan*, sir".

At the fringe of panic David grabbed the mike, keying it while speaking rapidly, "Hello? Hello? This is David Holbrook again, aboard *Skyoil-One*. We've got a very serious problem now. We seem to be under attack by a craft of unknown origin."

"*USS Lavan* here. Am I to understand that you are under fire?"

David hesitated only a moment. "It's possible. I didn't exactly see what hit us, I just saw one of our masts collapse." He described as quickly as he could the events of the past few minutes. Looking back up at the monitor showing the bubble, he saw the members of his crew and the two executives boarding the strange craft. "What the *hell* are they doing?" He then relayed that information to the Navy ship as well.

Releasing the mike for a second, he turned to the man standing behind him and shouted his name. The man snapped out of his reverie as he noticed David's glare.

"Get up there! Go by the gun locker and grab something, and be careful. See if you can find out what the hell's happening up there!" As the man ran out of the room, David looked back at the screen and realized it was already too late. All the men who had been on deck were aboard the bubble, and it was beginning to move away. Relaying this latest development to the ship, he released the mike.

"*Lavan* to *Skyoil-One*. We are proceeding at flank speed to your position. We have just detected a new radar contact within fourteen miles of your location. Our ESM report no radio emanations from this new contact, but it appears to be of immense size. Do you see anything to the south-southeast of you?"

David looked around the room. "You, John! Go to the lookout and see if you can see what this guy's talking about. Take the binoculars and a radio and call down with everything you spot." As the man rushed from the room, he met with the one who had gone topside moments before. The man entered the room and began, "Nothing doing, Mr. Holbrook. I got there too late, and they were..."

"I know," David cut him off. "I saw the whole thing up there." He pointed to the center monitor, which now showed only a vague blue light far away. The bubble was nearly out of sight.

David turned his attention back to the mike. "Hello, *Lavan*. Our crew members are now gone, apparently taken aboard that unknown craft. The thing seems to be heading basically south and now..." His report was cut short by a cry that came over the radio on the cabinet.

"My God! What the heck is that?"

David picked up the radio. "What is it? What have you got, John?"

The man's amazement was evident even over the small radio. "I don't know, Mr. Holbrook. I swear to God, it's the damnedest thing I've ever seen. There's an even bigger bubble than the one we saw. *A hell of a lot bigger!*"

"Where is it?"

"Basically south...south by southeast, I'd say. It lights up the whole damn horizon. The whole thing looks like it's glowing. I can't make out much detail or tell just how far away it is, but either it's pretty close or it's pretty damn big."

David again spoke to the Navy ship, telling them of what he had learned from John's report. There was a short pause, and then the voice of the commander came back on.

"Read you. That matches our bearings. We should be in range by mid-morning."

David mouthed a silent prayer and acknowledged the ship. After he signed-off, he handed the mike back to the communication operator. "Here, call up Shore and tell them what we've got. I'm going to run up and see what's got John so excited." He took one last look around the control center and headed up the passage.

CHAPTER TWO

L iam, one of the ISS's four flight engineers, turned to his crewmate and asked, "What's the payload this time?"

"Soil samples and seeds," Pete answered.

Liam remarked, "I never thought I would go all this way into space just to become a farmer."

"Yeah, well I've come all this way to be a damn shipping and receiving clerk," he said with a laugh as he switched his mike on in preparation for his part in the operation. "ISS to Houston Mission Control, Com check, over."

"Houston Mission Control, read you loud and clear, all carriers normal, over."

"ISS, roger-copy, commencing *Griffin* capture. Orbital velocity matched, all systems are go-green, over." Pete released the mike and gave his control panel a final glance.

"Houston Mission Control, have you on monitor, you are *go* for capture."

Everything was perfect—just another forty million dollar payload ready to be plucked from space, Pete manipulated the station's robotic arm to grapple the *Griffin*. One more minute of waiting, a few more twists of the arm's controls, and another day's work would be done. Gazing at the night-side of Earth behind the module, his primal centers still managed to get scrambled looking up at the ground. "ISS, roger— commencing capture." Pete leaned forward and looked up at Earth again. As he stared at the dark globe above him, something caught his eye. At first he wasn't consciously aware of what had made him attentive, but then it came again—a spot of light flashing for a moment off the surface of the Earth. He nudged Liam. "Hey…" He pointed to Earth.

Liam followed his finger. "Yeah, what is it you—huh? What the hell is that? It can't be like lightning. There are no clouds in the sky. It must be something on the surface, but all that is there is ocean." The flash came again. Both astronauts knew that there was nothing between them and the Earth which could be producing the light. The major cities along the eastern coast of America were also clearly visible, and from their location the two men could deduce all major land masses in the vicinity. The light wasn't near any of them.

Pete spoke to Liam, his eyes not leaving the viewport. "You see it, too?"

"Uh, yeah—I don't exactly know what it is, though. You?"

"Nope, are the scanners on?"

As quickly as he could, Liam shot his glance to the control panel, ensuring that the automatic cameras and receivers were activated, recording everything happening on the planet above them. "Yes, they're all on. I hope video's getting this."

"Me too. See if you can zoom in camera three on whatever that is. I want to get as much of it as we can, in case it's, um, important."

As Liam began working with the controls of the video recording system, the voice of Control came over the radio.

"Houston to ISS, ten seconds to capture."

"ISS, roger-copy—T minus five seconds, four, three, two, one, mark—I have *Griffin* by the tail. Orbital insertion is normal, all readings satisfactory, over."

"Control to ISS, concur, all readings normal. Tracking verifies capture. Well done, ISS."

"ISS, roger-copy." Pete looked through the viewport. The flash was now a dull glowing spot. He turned to Liam. "Did you get it?"

Liam confirmed, "Yeah, I got it for about fifteen seconds. All of it on zoom with camera three."

"Good. That should be worth looking at." He keyed the mike. "ISS to Houston, Schloesser here. Did you have any indication of an atmospheric disturbance just prior to *Griffin* capture, over?"

"Houston to ISS, wait one." There was a pause, and then the voice came back on. "Houston to ISS, there is no record of any major disturbance in the past hour. Are you having any problems, over?"

"ISS, no, no problems—just an observation. Immediately after T minus one minute we saw some sort of illumination. It appeared to be a white or yellow light of great intensity on the surface or low in the atmosphere. Best estimate of location puts it in the middle of the Atlantic, over."

"Houston, roger-copy. Did you record it, over?"

"ISS to Houston, yes. All automatic systems were fully functional, and we manually zoomed in camera three before the light dissipated. We still see the light, but the intensity has dropped off considerably. The total duration of the flash was approximately forty seconds, over." Pete looked at Liam, who nodded his agreement.

"Houston, roger-copy. We still have no communications concerning major disturbance, atmospheric or otherwise, but we will contact meteorology and Navy, over."

"ISS, roger-copy, over." Peter brought the robotic arm up and positioned the transport module onto the air lock's ring. Once in place it automatically screwed its ring into place and made the seal secure. A green light over the airlock turned on, indicating lockdown. "ISS to Houston, *Griffin* is secure, over and out."

CHAPTER THREE

Whatever the group had expected of the inside of the bubble, it wasn't what they saw. There was nothing there. No controls, no operators, no machines were visible. The inside of the bubble looked just like that; the inside of a bubble. It was the same glowing blue substance as the floor and the outside of the bubble.

When Tom went to a side wall and felt it, it felt the same as the floor. He considered the idea that the entire craft was one piece of material. For a moment he thought of asking Raval or one of the other of his captors, but a glance at their expressions made him withdraw the intention. None of the three seemed in the mood for questions.

The rest of the group was also looking around skeptically. Depending on their sympathies, they were all searching for the drive mechanism, the control center, the communication gear, or the weapons of the craft. None was apparent. The only feature of the large dome shaped room in which they stood was a smaller but identically shaped dome in the center. This one was only four feet high and six feet in diameter, however. It too was unmarked, just a scaled down version of their present location.

After an initial visual inspection of the room, Bob tried other means of gathering information about their location. He listened carefully, but as before no sound was apparent from the vessel. The only noises his ears could discern were those of the captives. Even the crew of the bubble was silent. They simply stood to themselves a short distance from the oil crew, watching without interest.

Bob stared at them. They seemed to be waiting.

The group didn't even have time to get bored or any more restless when their captors began moving again. They walked toward the far side of the circular room. Just then the wall parted in front of them—just as it had done on the other side.

Both Bob and Tom noted with surprise that the new door was directly across the dome from the first one. None of the men had moved very far from where they had entered. As soon as they were all aboard, the door had closed without leaving a seam or mark of any kind in the wall. The new door had appeared the same way, without warning or evidence of its existence.

The two subordinates walked out through the door and stepped to either side of it. There they stood, while Raval continued onward. The captives looked at each other with discomfort, waiting for someone to take charge. Most of them looked at Bob or Paul in expectation. Catching the stares, Bob glanced at Paul, shrugged, and said, "I think we ought to just wait. It shouldn't be too long before something happens. They were kind of in a hurry to get us here, after all."

He was right. Within a minute of Bob finishing his statement, Raval returned, walking behind another, older-looking man. The new fellow appeared to be of the same race as Raval and his compatriots. He was taller than most of the men from the oil rig, built a little on the slender side, and wore some sort of a robe that came to his ankles. It reminded Bob of the robes he'd seen worn by the Arabs when he visited their refineries. Those had been made of another material, but the idea was the same.

The man stopped in front of the group. He looked at them a moment, then asked, "Is there a leader of this group?"

The men looked at each other. After a short pause, Paul said, "Go ahead, Bob."

Bob stepped to the fore. "I guess I'm it."

The newcomer looked at him. "Welcome. My name is Atar. I am one of the elders of this city." He bowed his head ever so slightly. "I would first like to assure you that we do not intend to harm you or your friends. I apologize for the way you were brought here, but I am afraid we are in somewhat of a hurry to learn some things, and your construction was the closest place we could hope to get this information." Knowing no one had been injured, he added this last statement to reassure the group of their peaceful intent. "I trust none of you were injured?"

Bob shook his head. "No, nobody was hurt." He paused a moment. "Were you responsible for what hit us earlier?"

Atar nodded slowly. "Indirectly. It was a result of our actions. We regret any inconvenience it caused, and we will do what we can to compensate you for the damage we brought about. There are some things we would like to do first, though." Surveying the newcomers, he continued, "Please do not think of yourselves as prisoners. While it is true you cannot at this moment leave of your own free will, we will not do anything to bring harm to you in any way. In addition, we do not intend to hold you against your will for any longer than is absolutely necessary. As I mentioned, however, there are some things we urgently need to know."

Paul stepped forward. "Listen, that sounds very nice, and as long as we all stay reasonable about this, there shouldn't be any real trouble. I think we do have some right to know where in the hell we are, though." He swung his massive muscular arms around the expansive room and said, "None of us have ever seen anything like this. What's it made of? What's it for? And where the *hell* did it come from? There's no land anywhere close to our well, much less a fifteen minute ride away!"

After a dramatic pause, Atar looked at the floor then back to Paul. "I understand your confusion. I cannot answer all your questions just now. You would not believe me if I did. It will have to suffice to say that you were correct—until a short time ago, there was indeed no land near your site. As you can see this is no longer true." Atar turned to Raval for a moment, then back to the group. "Come. I will now show you some of our city. It is really quite an honor," he added with a grin, "you will be the first outsiders to see it in many, many years." Motioning to them, he walked out the door.

The first thing that caught the attention of the group as they left the craft was the size of the area outside. They had stepped out onto a balcony-like deck as wide as a four-lane highway. Looking outward, it was apparent that they were inside something that was bigger than anything any of them had ever seen.

Even though they had a clear view for about a mile, they could not see the sky. In fact, they were not, strictly speaking, outside. There was actually a wall around the entirety of the area in which they stood, and what was above them was definitely not the sky. It was blue, but that was where the resemblance ended. There was a glow suffusing everything. A glow the group had come to know well. It was the same light as that of the blue bubble.

Atar stood quietly as they took in the vista that lay below them. It was indeed a city, a big one. The buildings were primarily low, with few more than four stories high. Their vantage point was the highest spot in the visible area. Bob guessed they were about fifty feet from street level.

The city was full of action too. There were few vehicles, and none of the ones they spotted were very large. The streets appeared to be occupied by pedestrians and a surprisingly large number of animals. The pace of the city wasn't hurried, but there was a lot going on.

Bob leaned over to Tom and spoke from the corner of his mouth, "None of these buildings should be here, should they?"

Tom nodded. He too had noticed the apparent predilection of these people to take influences from any and everybody. He'd spotted examples of at least three distinct styles of architecture and innumerable combinations and permutations of them. There didn't seem to be any concept of chronological consistency about the city, either. A good portion of the visible metropolis was quite modern and new looking, although some of it had obviously been modeled directly after ancient Greece or Rome. Overall, it was a damn strange effect.

After a few minutes of letting the men observe the city, Atar moved to the front again. He raised his hand and spoke to the group. "I am sorry to limit your time for viewing our city, but it is necessary for us to now go to the Central Hall. There you will meet the council and be introduced to our leaders. It is there also that we will attempt to gain information about the situation in which we find ourselves. You will be able to ask what you wish of us, as well. Perhaps that will help quell some of the apprehensions you are experiencing. For now, let us go." He indicated for them to follow, and headed down the street.

Tom and Bob silently gazed as they followed Atar with the group of men from the rig. The more they looked around, the more perplexed they became with the apparent randomness of the city's design. While both knew that random appearance sometimes simply indicates a lack of understanding of pattern, there truly did not seem to be any rhyme or reason to the construction they were walking beside. Some buildings seemed to be modeled after those they had seen as examples of ancient architecture. Some would be quite acceptable on any given street in New York, and yet others resembled nothing either had ever seen before.

They walked for about a quarter of a mile before stopping in front of a huge building which appeared to be made of marble. It was the largest in the area, fronted by six caryatids at least forty feet tall. Tom noticed it was one of the older styled buildings, and smacked of bygone Greek influence.

Atar halted before the imposing structure and turned to the group. "This is our Council Hall. The best comparison would be, I suppose, to explain it as our county seat. It is in this building our government meets and makes decisions. I have brought you here so that you may meet the men who are the leaders of our city. They will have many questions for you, which I hope you will be willing to answer. At this meeting, some of your questions will be resolved. Let us now enter the hall."

Atar turned and climbed the stairs to the enormous front doors of the building. After only a moment's hesitation, Bob gestured his assent to the group and they went after the old man. Once inside the building, all the men were impressed by its appearance. It seemed, if possible, even bigger on the inside than the outside. It was obviously designed to impress. "Wait here," instructed Atar. "Someone will come for you momentarily. Please feel free to inspect your surroundings."

They started to mill about this foyer to the great hall with its massive pillars made of white marble etched in gold. The intricate cravings along the walls seemed almost alive, shaping the walls to the ceiling in a fluid motion of art and architecture to the finely polished floor. In the four corners of the great hall were statues. Assorted sizes and shapes depicted creatures of every mythical beast and women, many of them naked, but all were superbly made and intricately detailed. On one wall were pictographs similar to those found in the tombs of the pharaohs within the great pyramids, yet not the same—more modern dress and poses.

The thing puzzling one of the engineers was the origin of the light source. Nowhere was there a lamp or light fixture, yet everyone could see as if there were lights all about. The whole room, the great hall itself appeared to radiate, to glow with special brightness that illuminated the entire room.

The vastness of the room only served to intensify the isolation everyone was feeling. Tensions were mounting, and it wasn't long before they began to murmur among themselves. In fear or frustration, one crewman blurted out, "Why are we here? What do they want with us?"

Another cried out, "Who are they?"

One of the other engineers asked, "Where did they come from?" Their questions echoed around them as if to put an emphasis on their seclusion.

Noticing its radiance and subtle beauty, one engineer had drifted away from the crowd and was examining the rows of pictographs on one of the walls. Suddenly he blurted out, "I think I have the answer to most of our questions!"

The engineer named Steve pointed toward the wall and its section of pictographs. In a calm voice he explained, "When I started college I had thought that I wanted to become an archaeologist, until I realized there was no money in that career. At that time I took a course on Egyptology and studied hieroglyphics. That was before I got practical-minded and changed my field to geology, where the real money is. Anyway, these pictographs reminded me of the hieroglyphics found in ancient Egyptian tombs and the pyramids. They seem to describe a great holocaust, an erupting volcano, the island being covered and sinking, the rebuilding of a city, and their praise to God. And this one," pointing to the third segment of pictographs, "this one shows a woman, then a mermaid, then a woman again. I don't know what that means, but here…" as he pointed to a row of symbols in the center with a picture of a golden crown. "This symbol keeps repeating itself throughout. It's an old Greek symbol for kingdom and these are in Latin. I recognize the language but not the meaning."

Then the captain of the tanker spoke up saying, "That symbol you keep seeing that is always followed by these letters ᚴᚢᚼᛉᚠ means…"

"*Posidia*, lost then found, old yet new, the beginning of all things lies within you." All heads turned in the direction of the female voice that had clearly spoken the word Posidia. An attractive woman of youthful appearance had stepped into the chamber from a door now opened far down the hall. No one uttered a sound as all eyes fixed upon this fair-haired beauty. She was dressed in a short, light gown in the style once worn by the Greeks. The fabric of her garment swayed as she approached the newcomers. Her seductive steps caused her gown to gently caress her body at times, and to perfectly conceal her form at others. No one could pry his eyes from this living work of art.

Bob studied her shapely legs admiringly, reminded of the waitress back at O'Hare. His mind reeled with uncontrollable fantasies, thinking,

Damn, they go all the way up! Her unusual elongated frame only served to enhance her feminine appeal, adding fuel to Bob's lustful thoughts.

She stopped about four feet short of the group and stood in front of the radiating wall of pictographs. Gesturing toward the wall, but keeping her eyes upon this group of men, she said, "You are very observant and knowledgeable for *surface dwellers*. We have been observing you ever since you were brought into the city."

Just then Tom found his courage and blurted out, "Who is this *we* you are referring to, and why have we been brought here?"

Ignoring his outburst, with the turn of her wrist she caught the attention of everyone and pointed again to the wall saying, "Here lies the answer for those who care to use their minds, but in any case the council has assembled and I am here to escort you to the chamber where all of your questions shall be answered." With a flip of her hair she turned and began to walk back down the hall toward the open door where she first appeared. She strode with confidence knowing no one would try to harm her or take her hostage in order to gain their freedom.

They followed her as if hypnotized, focusing on the sway of her hips, her lanky frame, and long flowing flaxen tresses which draped down her shoulders and back. Stopping before a pair of immense doors, at least fifteen feet high and nearly as wide, she faced the group and said, "This is the meeting room of the Council. I realize you may be a bit apprehensive. Rest assured, no harm will come to you. The only reason for this meeting is to exchange information with you. There will be ten council members, and they will do no more than ask questions of your group. If you feel that their inquiries are too prying or personal, you may abstain from answering them. In all likelihood, however, you should find them remarkably uninteresting. Come," she said, as she led the men through the doors into the inner chamber.

It was even more elaborate than the one they had just left. This room was more suited to the domicile of a king of a wealthy nation than for a meeting room of a democratic council. There were scores of tapestries along the walls depicting scenes of strange and exotic creatures. In reference to what was depicted on the tapestries, Tom leaned over and whispered to Bob. "Whoever these guys are, they seem to share at least the same legends we do."

He'd spoken softly, but the acoustics in the room were apparently better than he'd assumed. At this comment, Atar turned and gave him a look. It was neither an expression of anger or surprise; it seemed to Tom to be one of amusement. The group was so awed by the ostentatious nature of the room's furnishing that it was several seconds before they even noticed the ten men seated around the table in the center of the room. Huge though the table was it still seemed small placed in the scale of the grand room in which it sat: the great council chamber of the elders of Posidia. The elders were the ruling class. Ten devoted men to decide the fate of their city state.

A gesture made by one of the elders toward the guards at the door was acknowledged by a slight bow of heads from each. Once the group was inside the chamber the two muscular guards posted at either side of the door slowly stepped outside into the corridor, pulling the massive doors shut behind them. Then each took up their positions. They had their orders, and these two would ensure that no one disturbed the council.

One of the men next to Tom caught his breath upon entering the room and uttered, "*Jesus!* What I could do with a shopping cart and fifteen minutes here!"

Tom mentally agreed wholeheartedly. There was easily enough wealth represented in this room to allow quite a few people to live their entire lives in comfort. In short, it was all damn impressive.

The room was quiet except for the echoes of their footsteps as the group made their way to the long marble table. Before them sat the ten men who ranged in age, by appearance, from their early twenties to well into their late eighties. Atar broke the silence. "I am the eldest and referred to by some as keeper of the heart of the city."

Paul snickered to himself and mumbled, "Big deal."

Tom glared at Paul as the rest of the group remained quiet, hoping that by doing so they would soon find out why they were here, what was to be done with them, and when they would gain their freedom.

Atar looked at each of the other seated councilmen in turn for a moment, and then turned to the gawking crew of the oil rig. "I see you are somewhat impressed by the accoutrements of our hall." There was a note of irony in his voice. "When you have completed your inspection, we will commence." At this, the waiting council nodded as one, then sat back patiently and waited. It wasn't long before the group began to feel self-conscious enough to sheepishly make their way to the chairs awaiting them at the near end of the huge table.

At first Bob wondered if someone would be left standing, but as he sat he noticed that the number of chairs present were equal to the number of the men in the group. When the crewmen had taken their seats, one of the councilmen lifted his hands to gain their attention. Like Atar, he was older than most of the group in appearance, with white hair above a handsome face, just beginning to show some effects of age. To Tom, he appeared to be a very well preserved fifty-year-old. His voice was deep and soft, but none of the group had any trouble hearing him.

"Greetings gentlemen, my name is Hercle." Raising his eyebrows and staring directly at Bob, as if addressing his remarks to him, he stated, "I trust you have not been distressed by your abrupt trip here?"

Bob half-shrugged, "No big problems yet, but I must confess that we're awfully curious about what exactly is going on here."

Hercle smiled and gave a nod, "Totally understandable. Allow me to bring you up-to-date concerning what has transpired in the last few hours for us." He turned to the man on his left and inclined his head slightly. The man nodded and looked at the blank wall behind the Council. The others did the same while the men followed their gaze. A collective gasp came up from the newcomers' end of the table as the entire wall dissolved into a fantastic view of the Earth which looked as if it had been taken from space. The continental shapes were quite distinct, and the shades of the various land masses and expanses of water were astounding in their clarity and variety. As the men watched enthralled, the view swooped in on the ocean between the continents of North America and Europe. Where everyone expected empty water, there appeared, as if a camera was zooming in closer, a small island.

Bob and Tom frowned. Both were well acquainted with the geography of the ocean in the area the screen was showing. After all, they had been poring over a navigator's chart less than three hours ago. The island they were looking at was not on any of the charts.

Looking at the face of each of the oil men in turn, and reading varying degrees of confusion and consternation in them, Hercle acknowledged their apprehension. "I understand your skepticism. It is true that there is no land mass at all plotted on the maps or charts you presently possess. I am afraid, however, that will have to change." He looked around at them. "Approximately four hours ago there was a very large disturbance under the sea, the center of which was located where the labeled spot is on this map." He indicated the wall behind him. "Your construction is, as you can see, a short distance to the north of this disturbance. This city, as you may have guessed, was very close to the center of the eruption."

Momentarily forgetting propriety Tom burst out, "Eruption? What eruption? There are no active volcanoes or faults for miles. The last recorded incidence of seismic activity anywhere near here was decades ago!"

"You are correct; inasmuch as there have been no natural cataclysms here for a very long time. However, we have had reason to believe that there was an event of very large and dangerous proportions in formation recently. Our leading scientists brought this to our attention and of the possibility existing of our city, and thereby our people, being destroyed by this catastrophic event. We decided to take action to prevent or ameliorate this occurrence."

Bob and Tom exchanged a look, each knowing what the other was thinking. The action required to offset a geological phenomenon like an undersea eruption or earthquake was, as both knew, of almost unimaginable scale. This man was speaking of performing an operation which few, if any, nations of the entire world would be capable of executing, even if they could foresee such an event. And neither of them thought foresight of this sort was possible. Not by the United States anyway, or any other country they knew of for that matter. Bob was beginning to formulate questions in his mind about these matters when Hercle began speaking again.

"You will be told more specifics as we go along. Allow me to present the major point of our story, however, to help you understand our predicament."

Paul glanced around again. *What the hell does any of this have to do with us?*

"This is, as you have perceived, a very old city. It is in fact older than any city in existence. Our people are a race descended from stock which has not been mingled with for many generations. That, perhaps, will help explain some of the physical differences between us," continued Hercle, ignoring Paul's intense glare.

Some of the crew nodded. The tendency to tall, slender builds among the city's people had not escaped them. Almost to an individual, the inhabitants they had seen were well over six feet tall, but appeared quite thin by normal standards.

"I hope I have not misled you too much by referring to this as a city," Hercle added. "In your terminology, it would probably be more accurate to regard us as a country. We are indeed isolated from any other people, though not as much now as before." He smiled slightly. "Before this day, we were separated by several hundred fathoms of water."

Looks of incomprehension greeted this remark. As the men mulled over his cryptic comment, he turned to a side door and made a small gesture with his hand. "Perhaps you are hungry or thirsty. It would please us if you would partake of some of our preparations. I think you will find our food and drink relatively close to your own. I hope you find it palatable."

During this speech, four young women entered carrying trays which looked too heavy for them to lift. The salvers, which were approximately two feet by three feet, fit well into the decor of the room in which they sat. They appeared to be made of silver, and Bob would have believed as much, if it were not for the copious quantities of food and drink each tray supported.

The young women too were well worth looking at. Tall, with slender but definitely feminine figures, any of them would have turned more than a few heads in any room. There were only minor differences in their appearance, Tom noted. They could easily be identified by observers as sisters. Their clothing aided in the resemblance. Each wore an identical light tunic of some sheer, unfamiliar fabric. They were cut quite short, and were only slightly longer than the girl's waist-length raven hair.

Acknowledging the high pressure stares of the foreigners only momentarily, the women set down the trays at intervals. Without distributing the food or drinks they again went to the door from which they had emerged and left. The eyes of every crewman remained glued to them until the door closed behind them. When the spell holding them was broken, the men turned back to the table and examined the trays placed before them, which had heretofore gone unnoticed in the radiance of the serving girls.

Before they managed to make a detailed examination, however, Hercle spoke once again. "Gentlemen, we would like to pursue this exchange, but we will first leave you to your own devices, if you do not mind. With your permission, we will take a recess in another room of the hall, and leave you to eat and drink in peace. Does that suit you?"

Bob looked at his compatriots. Most of them were staring raptly at the trays before them. It was obvious to him that they could use a break. In addition, he wanted a chance to discuss their predicament with the men, preferably without the members of the Council present. He addressed Hercle. "Thank you, that would be greatly appreciated. I believe we could use a moment to assimilate what you have told us. A break for dinner would be very nice." Anything familiar at all would be welcome at this point.

"Good." Hercle, Atar, and the rest of the Council rose. "Will an hour be sufficient?"

Glancing at the rest of the group and seeing no dissension, Bob nodded. "That would be fine."

At some unseen signal from Hercle, the ten men walked out a door at the rear of the room. As soon as the door closed behind them, the men dug into the food and drink on the tray. Just as Tom prepared to bite into an unfamiliar but delicious-looking fruit, vaguely resembling a tangerine, Paul's voice stopped him. "Hey! Wait a minute!" His yell drew the attention of everyone in the room. Looking around, then pointing at the fare on the table, he said, "How do we know this isn't poisoned?"

A few of the more edgy men dropped the food and drink as if they had been burned by it. Even the least cautious of the group looked at the variety spread on the table with suspicion. Sensing a possible crisis forming, Bob tried to think of a logical way to approach the problem. He didn't need to worry, though, because Tom's cooler head prevailed. "Listen," he began, and waited until he had everyone's attention. "Number one, if they wanted to kill us, they wouldn't have had to round us up and bring us to their city. You all saw what they did to the antenna mast. What would happen if they pointed whatever that was at one of us?" His challenging gaze held them. "Number two, even if they did want to kill us, why bother to poison us? There are a lot of faster, surer means of getting rid of people. Now, come on—you know as well as I do that this bunch doesn't mean us any harm, or they would already have done something to hurt us already. Instead, they bring us to city hall and give us a snack. A snack, I might add, that I can sorely use." He grabbed the nearest morsel and took a large bite out of it.

The group watched as one as he chewed and swallowed. When no violent reaction ensued, they one by one began to sample the various goodies on the table. Slowly at first, but with increasing vigor, they devoured the contents of the four trays.

Paul watched Tom as he ate. While he no longer voiced his suspicions, it was apparent he still felt less than assured by Tom's actions. Sitting back with his arms crossed, he refused to partake of the food or drink, all the while his dark eyes roving the room, as if expecting a sneak attack.

Tom hoped he wouldn't cause any trouble. Turning to Bob, who was consuming fruit and drink with fervor, he began to stare, waiting for a response.

Noticing Tom's focused expression, Bob paused his masticating and asked, "Well, what do you think?"

Tom replied, "About what?"

"What do you mean, 'about what'? Jeez man, look around you! Where is this place? Who are they? What do they want? Good God, aren't you even a little curious?"

Tom frowned and nodded. Staring into the distance and chewing absently for a moment before he spoke. "Where do you think we are?"

Exasperated, Bob said, "Where do *I* think we are? I'll tell you what I think! I have no frigging idea! None-zip-zilch-nada—nothing! That's what I think! I think these guys are from Mars, some bunch of weirdos from Zimbabwe. I think I have no damned idea what or who they are, or where we are. The whole deal is so fantastic that I can't even think of anything strange enough to make any sense of it!"

Tom nodded again, still looking far away. "Yup, I think you're probably right. I think this whole thing is so unlikely that there's no simple explanation. I do have a theory, though." He took another bite and chewed. "Do you want to hear it?"

"Of course, I'd consider just about anything! What's this theory?"

Tom told him.

CHAPTER FOUR

Bob gaped at Tom if he'd just grown another head. "You, uh—you serious? You wanna say that again?"

Tom munched with contentment. "Of course I'm serious."

"You mean as serious as can be expected in the middle of a snack on an island that sends out bubble-looking submarines and brings 'em back to a place where it doesn't seem to get dark? The construction is out of Alice in Wonderland, and the girls are, shall we say, tolerable to the eye." Bob pumped his eyebrows up and down salaciously; reaching across the tray in front of him he grabbed another cup of nectar.

Tom was still more than a little incredulous. He was not alone; two or three of the nearest crew members were casting suspicious, sidelong glances at the two of them.

"You may have a point. This whole thing has been pretty strange, but to call this place…" straining himself to utter, "…uh, Atlantis, well, that's really pushing it." He looked around the table for a response. No one met his eyes. They all seemed suddenly very intent on their meal, except for Paul.

"You're crazy! Certifiable, just because you don't know what's going on here or where we are is no damn reason to jump to any wild-ass conclusions. Don't tell me you're gonna believe those bozos? This has got to be some kind of fuckin' hoax."

Tom observed him calmly. "You got a better idea?"

Paul scowled and looked away. After a moment, he turned back. "Not right now. Give me a little time. I'm sure I can come up with something better than storybook plots." He lapsed into silence.

One of the men spoke up. "I don't care who these people are, they are mighty well off. Did you get a look at the buildings on the way here?

And *my gosh,* look at this room! Maybe they're crazy, maybe they're Communists, but they sure ain't poor." Most of the men around the table nodded in agreement. It was indeed obvious that whoever built this city, at least, was richer than anyone the group could imagine.

"I was noticing the artwork as we came in. Do you realize that some of it is more than a thousand years old?"

All the men turned to the speaker. It was Gerald Ahl, one of the more senior members of the group. He was the leading geologist of the crew. He added, "Now, I'm not exactly an expert, but I've picked up enough archaeology playing with rocks and such for the past thirty years to know old art when I see it. Those mosaics and a couple of the tapestries they have hanging in the room we entered, are either a millennia old or some hellacious good imitations."

"Valuable?"

Gerald snorted, "That's not even the word. Near as I can tell, that is the kind of stuff you can't buy at all at any price. Those are the sort of things museums get and keep. They're not for sale, and there are a very limited number of them, anyway. Besides, last I knew, the museums already have all the extant examples of that sort of thing."

Tom mulled this over while he absently ate a green fruit which resembled a tomato in appearance and angel food cake in texture. It was quite delicious, and he wondered where he could get some when he got home. He didn't wonder long, though, because Atar, Hercle, and the rest of the councilmen returned. They filed in and took their seats solemnly, without uttering a sound. As they seated themselves, the four servant girls reappeared and removed the remains of the food and drink.

When the table was cleared and the girls had left, Hercle began. "I hope you have enjoyed your meal. It is our wish that your minds be at ease as much as possible. Are you all now more comfortable?" He looked at the group.

"Yes, Hercle, I believe we're all better off for the break. Thank you for your hospitality. If possible, we would now like to ask you some questions also, as you can probably imagine."

Hercle half-smiled and nodded, "Yes, I am sure you do. First, let me introduce the members of our council to you. You have already met Atar, of course. To his right are Fronz, Marrick, Garth, and Tempest, who is the oldest of us." As each of the elders' names was spoken they acknowledged with a slight nod. Tempest, who Hercle referred to as the oldest, looked no more than eight or ten years older than anyone else at the table. Tom made a note to add asking about their actual ages to his list of questions.

While maintaining his gaze on the crewmen, Hercle continued, "Here to my left is Alstare, then Magyar, Vance, and lastly Mord. With the exception of Marrick, our youngest, we have all served as members of this council for a very long time."

The man introduced as Tempest spoke for the first time. His voice also was calm and quiet, but easily understood. "I will now attempt to explain a little further the history of our city. As Hercle mentioned earlier, this is a very old city. It is much, much older than any city now in existence. This we know because it was our people who founded the other truly old cities on this planet."

An unspoken feeling of shock greeted this revelation. Everyone at the table knew of Athens, Rome, and the other truly ancient cities of the world. They also had a good idea of the age of these places, and for the folk of this city to be present at the inception of the others meant a time period well over a thousand years.

Bob was the first to respond. "You're talking about a duration far greater than any single people on Earth has ever attained, you know."

Tempest raised an eyebrow. "No, actually, we don't know. This is one of the major reasons we need you. We have, for the past several millennia of this planet, been effectively isolated from any interaction with any of the other people on this globe. To be more specific, we have been living at the bottom of this body of water you call the Atlantic Ocean.

"I hope, in the telling of our history, you will become more sympathetic to our situation. An eon has passed since humans first stepped upon this planet. Many civilizations, cultures, and countries soon developed. Several were nomads; some were explorers and dreamers, and scientists. We came to this island in search of answers to the greatest questions mankind has ever asked, 'Why are we here?' In searching for that answer we made this island our home, and our cultural center. Through the wisdom of our forefathers, great bits of knowledge were discovered and stored here. We traveled throughout the world and everywhere we went we left our mark in that society. Always giving freely of the knowledge we obtained, we became a great center of trade. Medicines and treatment of ills was where we flourished. All the known sciences of all knowledge of the known world were stored in our archives; in that I must apologize for our forefathers. There was little warning of the holocaust that pulled us down into the earth's bowels, down into the murky depths of the ocean. When the holocaust came, all our stored knowledge went with us. It would take centuries for what we had gained to be rediscovered again.

"I said that all the sciences were practiced here and the treatments of ills are most known. Every manner of person came to us in hopes of a cure to a myriad of illnesses. Our forefathers felt that there must be a better way for humanity to live upon this planet—a way to better control his destiny and conquer the world. And so with that in mind our forefathers experimented with life itself. They felt that humans could be changed and made healthier, stronger, smarter, and live longer if only they could better adapt themselves to the world. We experimented and toiled many long years; years that turned to decades, and decades now into centuries. At first our attempts were crude and new creatures came into existence. Perhaps in your histories our creations have been recorded for all time. But know this; it was to better mankind that we sought such knowledge.

"While we became adept at the types of technology your civilizations seem to thrive on, it was not the thrust of our main efforts. Because of the relative scarcity of certain metallic elements on our particular land mass, very early in the development of our culture the focus of our scientific efforts became more and more centered on what we call life sciences: the reconstruction and use of the living cell."

"So you're saying you're a bunch of whacked out biologists?" interjected Paul.

Tempest shook his head. "The science of living things was simply the main thrust of our efforts, as the science of metals and atomic particles seems to be yours. We did attain, as I said, a degree of competence in making and utilizing metals and minerals, as you can see around you." With a wide sweep of his arm, he indicated the entirety of the room in which they sat. "In fact, I think you will find as you tour our city, many things our technologies have accomplished that yours have not."

"That's all very well and good," Bob put forth, "but you still haven't told us how you were cut off from the rest of the world. Or why you're back now."

"We were not, in all truth, cut off from the world. It was, to some degree, a matter of choice. While we were the oldest and most advanced society on this planet at one time, we were not the only one. We played a large part in the formation of many other societies also. As time passed the original intent of many of these cities and people became perverted or lost. The blood of the races and the mentalities of other cultures mixed with that of our people. Often within two or three generations, it was such a complete departure from our original strain that the individual bore virtually no resemblance to us.

"Our ancestors observed this phenomenon for many generations. As time passed, their alarm grew to near panic proportions. The existence of our homeland, here, was often completely forgotten or relegated to legend. Many of our achievements were viewed with fear or loathing by our distant descendants who had lost the knowledge to accomplish such things."

"What do you mean?" Tom asked, thoroughly confused by now.

"There are many examples in the room you entered."

"You mean those paintings and such?"

Tempest nodded. "Those are typical representations of some of our works. The creatures you see depicted on those drawings and paintings are not animals to be feared. They are simply the results of experimentation."

"Wait a minute! You're not talking about those mermaids, centaurs, and sphinx, are you?" Bob interjected.

"Yes, I am. We understand now that your people have recently begun to experiment with formation of life and the construction of cells and their basic design. Our scientists were far in advance of yours generations ago."

"Just what the hell were you doing to make things like that? Why would anyone want to create them?" Paul blurted out.

"I feel there is a cultural response taking place in you—one which reacts in a very negative way to anyone tampering with life. That was the reaction of the more primitive people too." He paused, looking carefully at them, as if deciding whether to continue. After a time, he did. "There was fear everywhere of what we were doing. No one dared attack us, but we were abundantly aware of the feelings about our work. The worst reactions by far came as a result of our modification of the structure of the human animal.

"We did indeed make humans—for that is what they were; they simply had bodies more suited to their environments or purposes. Some were capable of living in the sea, others the land or the air, and with bodies of great strength and speed. This was not even a difficult task for our technicians, once we learned the most basic building blocks of life and flesh."

Gerald spoke up. "Just what do you mean, bodies more suited? You mean you changed their bodies?"

"That is correct. The human organism, of course, is not adapted to live in all habitats, not naturally, that is. To be able to function success-fully in the ocean, it is necessary to increase its swimming ability. For it to be able to cope with life in the forests, where predators abound, it requires more speed. These attributes are severely limited by the present construction of the human body. Thus, we changed the body."

The light began to dawn on Tom. "You're saying those creatures in those pictures, they were real? That you really did make mermaids, and creatures, and the rest of them? Oh, my God..."

"You are right. Your attitude also reflects that of the Greeks and others of the time. Our first experiments were all with horses and goats. We created a horse with a horn in the center of its head and one with wings so it could fly. Next we applied these principles to man. We tried to give man the speed, grace, and strength of a horse only to create the centaur. By crossing man with a goat we gave him the ability to climb sheer cliffs and that brought us the satyr. As you can see, better adapting man to his environment was a difficult task to do. Many more experiments were needed to be done. Many more creatures were created.

"We did experiments with lions and eagles to get the character of strength and power of flight. This produced the griffin. From here we introduced a man and woman to determine if the sex of a human would make a difference. We found out that it didn't and created the sphinx. By now tales of our experiments were spread in many lands. They started to fear us for the work we did. Ignorance is an ugly thing. It makes intelligent beings fear the unknown or the unexplored."

This whole thing was getting to Bob. "Oh, God, not this!" Bob grabbed his head. The council members looked at him in surprise. Seeing their look, he glanced at Paul and spoke. "This can't be true. It's all myth! None of this can be real. This place just can't be what we call Atlantis?" Bob seemed almost overcome. He stared without focus into the distance, and then slowly seemed to rejoin them in the room.

∞ 44 ∞

Paul's reaction was almost diametrically opposite. He scowled ferociously and glared at the council members across the table. "Alright, you guys—just what do you call this joint? It does have a name, right?"

Tempest smiled. "Yes, it does. In fact, it has been called many things, Posidia for one. It has been so long, however, since anyone has needed to refer to us that there is no need to exhume the true name for our city. I think it will serve all our purposes best if you simply continue to refer to this place as Atlantis." The councilmen seemed satisfied at this.

"It is not easy for us to say just how old Atlantis is," Tempest continued, "because we were already quite advanced by the time other cities of significant proportions came into existence. Suffice it to say that many of your oldest legends and myths came about as results of our experiments and explorations. Not all of our products, however, were held in such fear or contempt. The result of one of our experiments became one of the most influential kings of the largest country in the continent you call Africa. He has, in fact, been immortalized, though that term has a very relative meaning, in stone for all to see."

The youngest-looking of the councilmen, who had been introduced as Marrick, spoke for the first time. "I believe the memorial to him still exists. The name your people have given it is the Sphinx."

"You are, of course, aware that the beings and creatures you speak of are now considered to be pure constructs of imagination," Gerald said, "and I hope you realize you're going to have one hell of a time getting people to believe this sort of thing ever existed at all."

"He's right," added Bob, "and even if you do, you will be facing attitudes an awful lot like the ones you had to deal with before. People still think there's something wrong with messing with the human organism. Most of us kind of regard it as a construct of God, and something that mankind was not meant to change."

The members of the council nodded. "We anticipated this possibility," resumed Tempest, "and that is another of the reasons we brought you here. We very much need to learn what we should do to gain acceptance in this time period. We must become acquainted with your ways and morals, so that we may help your cultures. And," he added, with a note of amusement, "perhaps you can help ours."

"Why us? Why now? What made you pick this time?"

"Our return to the surface wasn't exactly a matter of choice, either," Tempest admitted. "As we told you earlier, we were forced to take action to prevent the destruction of our city. One of the unavoidable side effects of this was that the sea floor beneath us returned to its original state, and we became a land mass again. In other words, it looks like we're going to have to remain up here."

The members of the crew again nodded in unison. The reluctant guests looked at each other. It was apparent that they shared the same thought. Just how would the rest of the world react to the appearance of this new group of strangers? And, perhaps more importantly, how would the Atlantians react to the rest of the world?

Gaining courage from Paul's earlier outbursts, Tom immediately asked, "Where can we go?"

Atar, getting a bit upset by the group's lack of patience, stood up and yelled, "Silence! Answers to your questions will be made to you soon enough! Until then, listen. You may actually learn something— *surface dwellers*." He said the words surface dwellers as if it were a curse or poison in his mouth as he spat the words out.

Atar then seated himself and the man called Hercle began to speak, "Some of you have read portions of our history on the main wall of the inner chamber. I am glad to see that some of our knowledge shared to your world so long ago has not been totally lost. Perhaps there is hope for your kind after all." His contempt for the surface dwellers could be felt in every syllable he spoke.

Hercle continued with his explanation, everyone listening, spellbound by what they were hearing. Everyone, that is, except Bob, whose thoughts began to drift as he became oblivious to the discussion taking place around him. Though he feigned interest, his eyes were locked upon the body of the unnamed girl in the skimpy tunic who had brought the group into the chamber earlier. She, however, paid him no attention as she had taken a seat in a chair just off to the left of the council's table.

Hercle gave a nod to a guard, and an animal resembling a small dog entered the room, yet it wasn't a dog, exactly. It startled everyone when it spread out its wings and flew across the hall toward the girl in the chair who most everyone almost forgot about. The dog or bird or whatever landed gently on her lap, stood up and licked her face, while the young woman blushed and held it firmly, stroking its fine fur and wings.

Tempest explained, "That is what we call a marfle; a pet to our children and a part of the legacy from our earlier experimentations."

Paul blurted out, "So you created monsters and pets, so what! What good did it do you?"

Annoyed by Paul's outburst, Atar rose and spoke asking, "What good is life if you do not live it to its fullest? We were fulfilling a dream so that humanity would not be limited to geographic or climatic changes. Why do you build ships if one's home is enough? Mankind is a creature. Exploring and traveling is as much a part of him as breathing!"

Tempest then continued, "As you have surmised earlier, this is Atlantis and we hold to a proud heritage. We continued our experiments, this time on humanity alone without introducing foreign matter into its being, but by changing that which he already possesses. We discovered parts of the body that secreted various substances into the body and felt that these secretions were the basis that regulated life. In one experiment, we increased the amount of secretion of one substance into a youth. That child grew well, becoming stronger and much faster than his peers, but continued to grow even larger, until he was twice the size of a full grown man."

"Giants," murmured Bob, his attention back into the conversation at hand.

"We knew that we were getting closer—then the great holocaust struck. Our soothsayers provided some warning. So we sent out four ships; one to the east, one to the west, one to the north, and one to the south in a hope that our civilization would not die. Much of our collective knowledge was placed within those ships, and to this day we are uncertain as to what happened to them."

Tom inquired, "What happened in your great holocaust?"

Mord stood up to answer. "We were most fortunate that day. Even our scientists can't explain precisely what happened, nor for that matter how it occurred that so many lives and most of our city became preserved. Some say it was a freak of nature, while others more religious claim that it was God's will. All we know of that day is what was recorded. There was an enormous storm which happened to coincide with the island's volcano erupting, but this wasn't just any ordinary eruption. Our island was originally formed by this volcano, as indicated by the three outer rings. Centuries before we discovered this island and settled upon it this land mass had risen and sunk several times before.

"Our scientists felt it reasonably safe to live here, assured that further eruptions would be most unlikely. There has been no volcanic activity here since our forefathers colonized this place, but on that fateful day many strange things began to happen. When the volcano erupted most of the inhabitants fled to places of safety within the city. The entire island shook as if its very foundation was being ripped apart. Tons of magma flew into the air and down its side. A large ditch had been cut into the earth around the city as part of its fortification, and as the lava flowed, it totally surrounded the city, filling this ditch. We were cut off with no place to escape.

"Once more the volcano erupted, but this time with such tremendous force that the magma fell around the city in sheets. By some mysterious freak of nature the storm's savagery blew and cooled the magma as it fell. Atmospheric pressures must have been immense because it caused the magma to fold over the city and the minerals in it to crystallize and change. An enormous geode was created. A perfect dome formed over our city as layers of this changing magma continued to fold over the geode dome encapsulating our city as the island began to sink. The coolness of the ocean caused the magma to solidify. We speculate that the increasing pressure of the deep combined with the sudden heat dissipation caused a further change in the minerals around the island, completing the formation of this outer shell, preserving the city and its inhabitants while trapping a breathable atmosphere inside."

Mord continued, "Before the holocaust, we used geothermal energy to heat our city, much as we do now. Some have said that our tapping into the earth's heat is what caused the eruption in the first place. After the quake and sinking of our city, our ancestors' scientists produced a chemical light source to calm the panic of its buried citizens. We had little hope."

With a wave of his hand Tempest made a gesture and Mord stopped talking. He then continued where Mord left off. "My great grandfather, who produced that light, also knew about the mixtures in the air—the different gases of life. He knew how to produce these gases in great quantities, and change those expelled by man into usable mixtures once more. He built an elaborate device that regulated and maintained the very breath of our city. In the centuries that followed, little has been done to change his original design because he had made it that well." There was obvious pride in his voice.

"They knew they were cut off and any attempt to leave their imprisoned city would cause the destruction that God or a freak of nature once prevented. Many medications had to be given to the population to prevent some from trying to escape. For an unknown reason, isolation caused some to experience great fear and an unusual urge to depart. Those persons were kept asleep while the work to find a way to escape their fate continued. The city was rebuilt using the changed minerals of what was once slate. Further experiments yielded energy cells for power, and new light sources were developed.

"Originally, we found power in the new light we developed, power enough to cut through solid rock. We discovered, by accident, while mining this changed mineral with our new power light tool, that in hitting the mineral at a certain angle it would cause the entire piece to glow bright. We now use it as our primary light source."

His hand went over a light control and the illuminated wall behind him went opaque. "By changing the central crystal of our power light, its strength and use changed: green for light, blue for heat and cooking, and red for power and the ability to cut stone, metal, and even flesh. Later, through much experimentation, we learned that with further refinements we were able to use it as an aid to surgery. The weapon used to persuade you to accompany our guard force was also such a device. Now you know the full meaning to the first panel in the great hall."

Feeling that now would be a good time to ask about the pictograph, Tom inquired, "What does the center panel of the wall mean, the one with the woman and mermaids pictured on it?"

"Mermaid—oh, you mean the Aquarian!" remarked Tempest. "As I said, our ancestors continued to try to find a way to escape their watery tomb."

Having some of their questions answered, Atar signaled to have food and drink brought into an adjoining room where the outsiders would again be able to satisfy their hunger and quench their thirst. After their meal, wine was provided for all the surface dwellers. Bob eagerly accepted this and drank deeply from his goblet. The others soon followed suit and as each finished their drink a sudden slumber came upon them. The wine had seemingly been drugged.

Atar had the guards and servants bring the slumbering captives to separate sleeping chambers located elsewhere in the great hall. Hercle came to Atar inquiring, "All the captives have been put to bed and guards are set outside their doors. What shall we do with them when they awake?"

Atar pulled at his beard and mused for a moment. Finally he replied, "There is so much we do not know about the surface world and we must prepare as best we can for what may happen when the rest of the surface dwellers learn we have risen. Tomorrow we shall bring three of them before the council to question them. The others may go about the city, but must be escorted. Have my daughter and her friends be their unobtrusive escorts. Perhaps they may learn more about them that way. Send four patrols out about three leagues away from the island, and have them report of any new arrivals in our waters. They are not to make contact, but if any surface dweller should get within half a league, capture them and bring them before the council for interrogation."

Hercle replied, "Your will be done." He then turned and departed down the corridor.

Atar called to his daughter who had been waiting patiently in her chair near the council's table. As she approached, the marfle flew out of the chamber leaving the two alone. She said, "I know what you want done. I and my friends shall accompany the strangers and show them around the city." Changing her tone to that of confidence she continued, "We shall find out about the surface dweller's world and what can be expected."

Hugging her, Atar smiled, looking down upon her deep blue eyes and innocent looking face, and thought, *I am so very proud of you.* Looking up to his aged, wise face and soothing eyes, she sprouted a smile and hugged him back. Shifting away to break his embrace, she turned and walked toward her bed chambers. With a sign, Atar turned, and with a gesture summoned the two remaining guards to accompany him to his room. As he entered, the guards turned and positioned themselves outside his doorway on either side.

CHAPTER FIVE

Six hours later Hellena awoke and two supple, long haired young women entered her room. One attendant brought in a tray of soap, perfumes, brushes, and a towel and the other carried a skimpy tunic. Hellena motioned to the one with her gown and instructed, "Awaken Samantha, Sara, Serena, Sharon, Sheba, Sue, Thell, Theresa and Tina. Have them meet me in the dining hall in one hour. Ensure that food and drinks have been prepared for us."

Bowing, the first servant departed and slipped away through a side entrance while the second attendant drew the princess' bath. Undoing Hellena's bed clothes and letting them fall to the floor, Hellena stepped out of them, and went down the steps that led into the steaming, clear water. Setting upon a sunken seat she waited for her attendant to join her. After removing her own tunic, the servant placed her sandals to the side then slipped into the large tub alongside the princess. With soap and sponge her servant meticulously started to wash the princess' back, gently rubbing the night's sleep from her body. Hellena turned toward her, as she had so many mornings before, allowing the rest of her torso to be cleaned.

By this time her other handmaiden returned indicating that it was nearly time for her to meet with her young girlfriends. Upon hearing this, the attendant in the tub quickly sponged off the princess. As Hellena climbed out of the tub the other servant grabbed a towel from the nearby table and dried her off. Crossing the room to her bed, Hellena waited for what remained of her morning ritual.

The bather quickly dried herself off and took one of the bottles of perfume from the tray she had brought in earlier. Walking over to the princess' bed, she opened the bottle of perfume and splashed some of its contents onto Hellena's breasts, neck and shoulders. She then went to fetch the princess' tunic, brought it to her and helped her to arrange it upon her body. As Hellena shifted the tunic around into the proper position, her handmaiden then took out a brush and began to comb the princess' fine flaxen hair. Taking a last look at herself in her mirror, Hellena, now satisfied with her appearance, got up and stepped out of her room and made her way down to the dining hall. The one attendant then put on her own tunic and with the other's help began to pick up the bedchamber and make it tidy for when the princess returned.

Hellena felt like a new woman. With a lively spring in her step she entered the dining hall where her girlfriends had gathered and were discussing with one another the possible reasons why they were all called to this meeting. There was an assortment of food spread out on the table. The moment the princess sat down, one of the attendants promptly poured her a glass of juice. Then Sara spoke up, directing her question to Hellena. "Why have you had us awakened at such an early hour? Are there really surface dwelling men here in the citadel?"

The princess smiled and answered, "Yes, there are, and before you ask, they are very handsome!" A giggle came from a couple of the younger girls, but hushed when the princess turned and looked at each of them. Hellena explained, "That is why I had you all awakened. During the night, after most of the city had gone to sleep, one of our scoutcraft had located a structure near our island and brought these men here. They were questioned and given answers to most of their own curiosities, then they partook of our wine which put them to sleep; they were placed in private quarters and shall awaken soon enough. My father has asked me to get your help in a plan to obtain more information from them.

"Three will be sent before the council this morning for formal questioning. The others will be allowed to walk about the city freely, but with an escort. We will be their escorts. My father wants us to find out all we can about the past fifty or so years of the surface dweller's history. He feels that these strangers might be more receptive to the curiosities of women, and wishing to impress us, tell us what we need to know in order to better defend our home. None may go to the waterfront area, but anywhere else will be allowed.

"Use your imagination! Find out what you can, anyway you can. This information is vital to our survival now that we have surfaced. Even the elders only have records of the time when we too were surface dwellers, and beyond that the many times we have attempted to make contact, but none of this tells us enough to know what to expect in the next few days or perhaps even hours."

Hellena took a swallow of her juice before continuing. "Are we still a superior nation, or have our surviving ancestors given them the knowledge that now enables them to surpass us? Any detail, no matter how small, may be important. Once you've finished eating I will have the attendants take you all to the stranger's chambers in the private quarter. We will all meet back here in four hours. At that time the outsiders will be allowed to eat and refresh themselves as we tell what we've discovered to the council."

Quietly pondering all that the princess had told them, Serena asked, "Is there anything we are not to tell them of our city or ourselves?"

The princess quickly replied, "No, nothing. The freer we are with our information the freer they may be with theirs. I just wouldn't offer any information unless they ask a question."

"Sounds like fun," Sara giggled.

With a smirk the princess added, "The brown-eyed Adonis, who calls himself Steve is mine." Hearing this all the girls broke out in laughter.

Though they all knew the potential peril their sudden surfacing had placed them in, and the damage that had been caused by their violent upsurge only hours earlier, they all seemed at ease with the task set before them. With a gesture from the princess, the servants cleared away the table as the attendants began to escort the young women to the private quarters. Precisely fifteen minutes after each girl entered the quarters of their assigned man he began to stir.

Tom stretched and yawned in his bed, scratching the back of his head, then jerked suddenly when he remembered that the last thing he had done was drink a goblet of some sweet tasting wine. His thoughts raced. *They must have drugged me—uh us—yeah that is what must have happened. Where am I now and what happened to the rest of the crew?* He jerked again, startled at seeing a women sitting across the room from his bed, but before he could utter a sound the girl started to speak.

"I was beginning to wonder if you were going to wake up at all! I am Serena, and I have been instructed to be your guide this morning. I shall try to answer any questions you may have, and if you would like, take you anywhere in the city." Pausing to see if the stranger comprehended what she was saying, she mused aloud, "My, aren't you a handsome man!"

In Steve's room, he easily recognized Hellena as the quiet girl in the corner of the council's chamber who owned that queer-looking dog. He sat up and noticed also that his clothes had been neatly folded on a chair next to the bed. "How did I get here? Who took my clothes off?" he asked in bewilderment.

Hellena answered sarcastically, "My, my, we are very grumpy when we first wake up, aren't we? It appears that you and your fellows cannot hold your wine. You all passed out after drinking only one sip, and there was so much more we wanted to discuss with you."

"Never mind all that!" he replied angrily. "Who took my clothes off? Was it you?"

"Ha, ha, ha, ha," she laughed aloud. "I assure you that it was not I. We have attendants for that. One of them disrobed you after the guards carried you here from the dining hall. Now hurry and get dressed. There is much I want to show you, and much I wish to learn of your ways."

"Well, the first thing you need to learn is to turn around and not stare at a man when he's getting dressed," he said blushing. "I hardly know you."

Letting out a girlish giggle, Hellena turned her back to him saying, "As you wish."

Steve stood up and rapidly dressed. "Alright, you can turn around now."

With a bemused, seductive look on her face, Hellena turned around, a finger to her lips as she smiled. "Your clothes do seem confining. How can you be comfortable in them?"

"They're plenty comfortable enough for me," but as he said that his eyes started to trail down her lanky form from her face to her long, slender neck, to the cleavage her tunic amply revealed, then down the curves of her satin-caressed body, past her rounded thighs, and to her exposed silken legs. Only then did he notice the delicate sculptured sandals she wore. Turning his attention to her thighs, he realized that he was staring and quickly brought his eyes back to meet hers.

She was still smiling, and taunted, "Like what you see?"

Steve blushed again, mumbling gruffly, "I thought you had some things you wanted to show me."

Taking his hand, she turned and led him out of his bedchamber and into the hall. Turning left, she led him through a corridor passing more such chambers. Noticing the puzzled look on his face as they passed the other rooms, the princess quickly stated, "Your friends should be awaking soon. Each has an escort and is free to join us whenever they wish." Continuing on, they came upon a large, guarded door. With a slight gesture from the princess, the guard opened the heavy door allowing them entry into what appeared to be a market place.

Inside his room Bob had just awakened, and being a lot less shy than Steve, when his escort introduced herself, he did not hesitate to get out of bed and walk toward her. With little regard for his nakedness, he took one of the girl's hands, her eyes opening widely in amazement from the boldness this man demonstrated, and pulled her to him while wrapping his other arm around her waist. Looking deep into her eyes, he saw neither fear nor excitement, so he pressed his lips against hers and kissed her passionately. In the back of her mind she remembered that Hellena had said to find out anything about these strangers she could, in any way open to her, so she returned his kiss allowing her passions to rise. As she arched her head back and shook her long, gold, silken hair behind her. He kissed her mouth, nibbled on her lips, and down her neck.

Bob led her to his bed, slowly lowering himself onto her. His lips roamed, kissing her on the neck, licking behind her ears, and on her lips once more. Bob pushed his tongue between her pursed lips and pried her mouth open so that his tongue could swirl with hers. After another long kiss he broke their embrace, gliding his face back to her ear. Upon licking it again he could hear her breathing pick up deeply, rasping with excitement, as he continued nibbling on her ear lobe. She let out a low moan of pleasure. It wasn't long before Bob's hands were all over her body. With one he rubbed her back through the silky material of her skimpy tunic, and with the other he made his way under it to cup one of her firm breasts. As their passions rose, Sue was not unaware of his excitement either, for his maleness was pressing into her side.

Before Bob could protest, she thrust upright, breathing heavily with excitement as if trying to catch her breath, breaking their loving embrace. Bob thought she was going to depart and leave him to himself when she surprised him by reaching to either side of her tunic and pulling it over her head to reveal the perfectly formed firm body of a woman in her early twenties. She then leaned back into his embrace, kissing him passionately, resuming the excitement both felt just moments before.

Steve and Hellena walked slowly through the streets of the city. He noticed that all the buildings were made of the same material, as were all the rooms of the citadel, each illuminating brightly. He asked, "Is the entire city made of this stuff?"

She answered with a question of her own. "Yes, don't you have such stone as this? What do your people use to make their dwellings and to light their rooms?

Steve was feeling hungry and answered her by saying, "If you find us some place to sit and eat, I'll tell you."

Passing the various shops of the market area, the two continued on down the hill into the outskirts of the city where they saw some huge men sifting through the rubble of some of the damaged buildings. "They are Soschatch," answered Hellena passively. "Their job is to maintain the buildings in repair. They are the only ones capable of lifting the massive slabs of rock used for the walls. As you can see we have suffered much damage when our island was torn from its roots at the bottom of the life waters, and hurled to the surface. The volcano is active once more. It is said that when the island sank the volcano was put to sleep."

Steve interrupted, "What caused your island to surface anyway?"

Thinking for a moment how to answer, the princess turned away then back to face him, indicating that they should sit down. After seating herself, she looked deep into his brown eyes and began to recite her reply. "Our scientists predicted that an enormous earthquake would soon occur that would devastate the city and possibly destroy it. It was suggested that if pressure was released down the fault line at a spot away from the city, the potential catastrophe might be averted."

At that moment a waiter from the cafe came to where the two

were seated and interrupted, "Excuse me, princess. May I take your order?"

Startled by what he just heard, Steve blurted out, "You're a princess? You never told me that. In fact, I don't even know your name."

Acting coy, the princess replied, "My name is Hellena. Do you always follow strange women around if they lead the way?"

Steve remained silent, flustered by not knowing right away how to respond. Taking a defensive stance, he answered, "No-o-o." He then quickly changed tactics by demonstrating his charm. "I mean to say, I don't follow women around unless they are as lovely as you."

It was Hellena's turn to blush. She liked the way Steve spoke, and then stated, "It isn't important that I am a princess. We all have our station in life and duties we must perform."

"Are you performing one of your duties now?" Steve asked bluntly.

Before the mood changed, and she allowed him to become defensive, Hellena gazed into his smoldering eyes then turned her attention to the waiter. "My friend here is hungry. I think he would like a sandwich, and perhaps a—a goblet of wine."

Thinking about what had happened the last time he drank their Atlantian wine, Steve hastily interjected, "No, no wine for me."

The princess smiled. "Very well then, bring him some juice."

"As you request, princess," replied the waiter who departed before Steve could acknowledge Hellena's choice of beverage.

Now that the waiter had left, Hellena went on with her explanation of how the island had reemerged. "As I was saying, a work force of Aquarian scouts were assembled and given the most powerful maser we have ever built. Its power came directly from one of the scoutcraft. They were given the precise location and angle to set the maser; and, using it, drilled a hole along the fault line in hope of relieving the fury beneath before it tore apart our city. It was a very dangerous and daring task. At worst, we expected to cause the birth of a volcano at that location. Instead, we awakened that which formed our island thousands of years before. The end result came when the volcano erupted, thrusting our island abruptly to the surface. It caused much panic and damage, but fortunately few lives were lost. We had prepared well."

Steve nodded slightly while thinking, *Then that must have been what caused the tidal wave. Anything as large as this island coming to the surface as fast as she claims could easily cause a tidal wave.* Lost in his thoughts, he didn't quite hear anything else she was saying until he heard her say, "Steve, Steve, are you all right? Is something wrong with you? Shall I get help?"

Startled, Steve said, "No, no. It's just that I was thinking to myself about what you just said."

"What were you thinking?"

"Well, a couple of hours or so before your scout ship captured us, the rig—uh, oil rig where I work was hit by a tidal wave, and we had hoped to locate its cause." He mumbled to himself, "I guess we did." Changing the subject to another curiosity he continued, "You never did give me a good answer about those—those Soschatch. Why are they so large? They are Atlantians like you, aren't they?"

She appeared to be puzzled by his question, so he concluded, "You don't know? Atlantis is a name a Greek philosopher and scientist named Plato called your island over two thousand years ago—so anyway are they Atlantians, like you?"

"I do not know any such Plato. I only know this place as home. Perhaps in our past it was called Atlantis. This I do not know, but to answer your question—yes and no. Yes, they are of this place you call Atlantis, and no, they are not like me." With a snobbish tone to her voice or one filled with self-pride, she continued, "They are Soschatch, bred and created by Oman, the one who controls destinies, to work as builders of our city. They know no other work."

Slaves! Steve thought to himself.

Hellena grew a bit angry and snapped, "Not slaves—workers! We all have our appointed crafts. They maintain the city. They are strong of body and weak of mind. We care for their needs and they care for the city's structure. Don't you have your own specialists?"

Steve's mouth fell open in astonishment. How could she know he was thinking slaves? He didn't speak it aloud.

Hellena now knew one answer. The surface dwellers were limited to speech for communication.

CHAPTER SIX

"ISS—Houston Mission Control."

"ISS—Aye."

"We have you at 350 kilometers and holding, about to pass over Atlantic Ocean. On my mark it will be T minus ten minutes to intercept point with luminous phenomenon —mark!"

"Mark-Aye-Copy-Check T minus ten minutes to intercept point."

"ISS—Houston, on this approach Control wants you to use the Big Eye and transmit pictures to Ground Control."

"ISS, copy. Big Eye is tested and ready. Liam is on station and ready. All systems green-go. On my mark T minus five minutes and counting—mark!"

"Houston, copy, awaiting your transmission."

Pete turned to Liam, "All set, chum? They sure got interested in what we saw after the first set of pictures."

"Yeah, I know. Extending our time on station another hour." Liam paused to look at his counter. Keeping his eye on the device, he said, "T minus thirty seconds on my mark—mark!"

"Mark—Aye," Pete noted.

"Give me power to the infrared camera," ordered Liam.

Pete flipped a switch and energized the infrared system. "Why for?" asked Pete.

"I've just got a hunch," remarked Liam. Turning his attention quickly to the counter, hand posed on the camera controls, "T minus ten seconds—mark, nine, eight, seven, six, five, four, three, two, one. Systems are on and running. Picture is clear."

"ISS—Houston, we are receiving video. Image is clear, good work."

"We copy Houston. All systems green-go." In a few minutes time the little speck of an island came into view, and Liam threw another switch on his control counsel. "Houston—ISS, systems are now on full automatic." As he reported this the Big Eye's lens turned and lengthened to magnify the image size 1,200 times. Liam checked his monitor and called to Pete, "Looks like an island to me. A good sized one from the image's clarity. It's oddly shaped though. Has a volcano chimney toward its northern side, and a large dome shape just below that."

"How can that be? There aren't any islands charted at these coordinates!" exclaimed Pete.

"I don't know, but come see for yourself." Pete got up from his station and floated across the cabin to where Liam was seated. Liam pointed to the image on his monitor and said, "See what I mean?" Pete didn't answer. He just stared at the monitor and thought of a reply.

After about fifteen minutes of the Big Eye noisily adjusting focal lengths, ground control called back. "ISS—Houston, we've lost contact with the island. Image lost, returning control to manual. Secure system, and prepare for further instructions."

"ISS—Aye copy." Liam flipped a few switches. "System secured, awaiting instructions." Pete returned to his station with Liam right behind him.

Back at Houston Control the images sent from the International Space Station were being studied with intensity. The data gleaned and confirmation of the existence of this new island was sent to Washington D.C. The Navy Department received the information and disseminated it to all Fleet Commanders. In Norfolk, Virginia, Admiral Hayes noted that this new island was located near the site of the damaged oil rig that the *USS Lavan* had gone to assist. He concluded that the island's sudden appearance could account for the tidal wave that damaged the rig. Since all this seemed to explain each event, he had his yeoman file this new information away until a more complete report could be obtained from the *USS Lavan*.

CHAPTER SEVEN

Paul, Greg, and Manny, the pipe fitter, were awakened and brought before the council. Atar began, "I hope you are well rested. There is much we would like to discuss with you. We would have talked more with you last night, but alas it appears our wine is too strong a drink for your kind." Atar had put that familiar half-smile on his face as he continued, "Your other friends are being well taken care of, I assure you. My own daughter and her friends have taken them on a tour of our city. Ah! Forgive me. I have caused you to assemble here and have not given thought to the fact that you might be hungry." Directing his command to the closest servant in view, "Food, bring these men some food! Some bits of cheese, fruit, and spiced meat for their breakfast." The servant bowed, turned around, and was off before any of the men realized that it was breakfast time and that they did feel a bit hungry. "Now if we may continue, I believe you still have some questions you wish to ask," continued Atar.

"Now look here!" Paul shouted angrily, pointing an accusing finger at Atar. "First, your men forcibly kidnap us and destroy part of our already damaged rig. Then we're taken to this place, where no place should be. You claim that this is the lost city of Atlantis, and that you are the descendants of the original inhabitants of this island, and now you want *us* to just sit down and discuss this over breakfast, calm and contented, as if this sort of thing happens every day—*Bullshit!*"

"Believe me, I understand your anger, but the fact remains that we both are here at this present time, and we both have questions that need to be answered," Atar replied, while looking directly into Paul's smoldering eyes. "I think that it would serve each of us better if I were to answer your immediate questions first. This way you may feel more relaxed in your present surroundings, and then be able to answer a few of our questions." Atar glanced at the others of the council, who for the past few minutes were sitting quietly while Paul and Atar were playing verbal tennis.

Just then two of the serving girls Greg recognized from the previous night brought in trays of food and drink as Atar had commanded. Graciously accepting the food, Greg and the other two hungrily dug into the fare. Greg relished the spiced meat, eating it with fervor. After consuming his fill, he felt a little more relaxed and decided to take Atar up on his offer and ask some questions that had been perplexing him since this whole episode started. Turning toward Atar, Greg began, "If you are Atlantians, how come you haven't made yourself known before now, and how come you speak perfectly good English?"

Tempest looked about the council before turning toward Greg to answer his question. "The fact of the matter is that we did seek out the surface dwellers of just a little over seven decades ago. Our scoutcraft was coming alongside a ship when a submersible launched some sort of swimming weapon toward our vessel, destroying it utterly. We decided then and there that your kind was too barbaric to attempt further communications with, so we determined that self-imposed isolation would be the best route for us to take."

World War II, Greg thought.

"As for learning your language, that was easy. Some of the crystals from our mine, we found, when exposed to the energy of the maser at reduced power levels would vibrate and produce sound. Further study of these crystals showed us that by varying the amount of energy into them different sounds were produced."

They'd learned to make a crystal radio, Greg speculated.

"Then in one such experiment we picked up what we later learned to be a broadcast carrier signal. Since then we have been monitoring your transmissions and soon learned all your known languages including the one called Crypto which seems to change with each usage."

Greg blanched. *My God!* Greg thought, *what they must know! All those secret messages. All those different languages.* Holding back his amazement, Greg asked another question, "What do you use as a light source? I mean, I look around and I see nothing burning or any other apparent light source other than that some of the walls glow."

Once more Tempest was the one who answered. "That same maser that we used to get you to board our scoutcraft and to receive your broadcast signals in another form is what we use to make light. I'll demonstrate this for you." Reaching for the control crystal at the base of the council's table, Tempest placed his hand over it and the panel behind him grew dim. Touching the crystal again then raising his hand from it slowly, the panel grew brighter and brighter until it was the brightest object in the room. Greg just fastened his eyes upon Tempest's every move and gesture to try to figure out just how the thing worked.

Tempest explained, "By touching this crystal I become part of the circuit from which it works, and by moving my hand away from the crystal the field of the force surrounding it allows it to grow stronger. This allows more energy from the maser embedded in the wall to be focused on the sheet of crystal which the wall section is made from. This then transfers the light from the maser, through the crystal, making the section glow brighter." At that, he tapped the crystal once and it resumed the brightness of the other wall sections. "Don't you have such devices where you come from? How do you produce light?" he inquired.

It was Paul who broke the silence and answered Tempest's question. "No, we don't have any such thing. We use a vacuum-sealed, clear glass bulb with a filament of tungsten in it which we apply an electrical charge through. The wire filament then glows brightly, producing light." Remembering some articles he had read about lasers used as tools, weapons, in surgery, and for communication, Paul continued, "We have other devices similar to your maser that we use as weapons and for communication. We also have a network of satellites hovering over the planet in fixed orbits containing such devices and other equipment which can scan the earth's surface and locate any ship or underwater craft. By now your island has been detected and a fleet of battle ships have been deployed to this very spot. Our satellite system can also focus that energy beam at any fixed location and destroy it. We call our system *Star Wars*, and to this date yours is the only country foolish enough to kidnap Americans."

Greg knew enough about Star Wars and other satellite projects from the newspapers to know that Paul had a hint of truth to his boasting, but most of what he had just said was more Paul's fanciful imaginings. Greg thought to himself, *What does Paul hope to gain by telling such a bold-faced lie? Whatever it is, for now I'll go along with it and see.*

Tempest stood up, angrily looked into Paul's eyes and retorted, "So a battle fleet is on its way here now, is it! Why doesn't someone use that Star Wars weapon and destroy us now, as you have said?"

Paul could not answer. He was trying hard to maintain his poker face and conceal any false expression that might give away the fact that he had just lied. Just then Paul had an inspiration. "Because there are Americans here, and we don't bomb our own people."

Continuing the verbal assault on Paul, Tempest went on, "Besides battleships and Star Wars are there any other forms of defenses that you *surface dwellers* have? What other modes of transportation do you use to travel the planet? Who or what nation is in control of the world? Is the planet still at war?"

Paul was getting frustrated by all these questions. Greg and Manny were in shock by the way Tempest was antagonizing Paul when just moments before they were being treated like regal guests. While all this was going on, the council members were complacently sitting back with their attention seemingly on Greg and Manny. They seemed completely indifferent to the discourse between Tempest and Paul. Greg was getting confused by the whole thing.

Paul gritted his teeth and replied, "We have land-based missiles and rocket-launched nuclear weapons, an army of millions, and jet fighters that continually patrol the skies for defense. We have several forms of transportation. By land we use a subway system and hover-craft, by water ships, by air jet planes and supersonic transports; in space we have starships, intergalactic scramblers to teleport from galaxy to galaxy. There is no war on this planet, and the war of the Jetties in quadrant Sigma Twelve has been over for nearly a century. No one person or nation rules the earth. There is a ruler on each continent and his representative is found at the United Nations building in New York City in America!"

Greg and the crewmen didn't know what to think of the fabrication Paul just told.

Atar looked to the council members to either side of him and exchanged glances, then turned to the two verbal battlers and spoke in a loud commanding tone, "That is enough!" Then the familiar calm voice and knowing half-smile returned to his face. "Again let me apologize for your inconvenience, and thank you for your time."

Paul's composure returned to him as Atar continued. "We now have most of all the answers we need to prepare for any encounter. You are now free to roam about the city. These three servants," pointing to the three girls who had earlier brought in the food, "will be glad to escort you around the city." Without uttering another word, Atar turned and departed the great hall with the other council members following behind him.

"Damn!" Paul spat as he shifted to face the other men. "I hate that guy. He gives me the creeps with his smug, know-it-all attitude."

"Yeah, I wouldn't mind belting him around the room myself," Manny said in agreement.

At last calmed down, Paul continued, "Well, I guess we might as well take them up on their offer to explore the city. Who knows what we may find out? Maybe we'll even find a way out of this hole."

The trio gathered their escorts and departed the great hall and went into the city. As they wandered about they saw these very tall man-like creatures moving large pieces of splintered stone around and doing what appeared to be repair work on the buildings nearby.

"Looks like they suffered a lot of damage too, if you can believe this whole story about Atlantis, a volcano shooting them up to the surface, and Aquarians," Paul said, scoffing. "Yet what bothers me the most is here we are and here they are on an island that I've never seen on any chart, and I've been working around these waters for going on twenty years."

One of the members of this ill-fated group decided to set into words his thoughts, "Do you think that they'll send out a search party for us?"

"Oh, hell yes!" reassured Paul. "Just before we were captured I had the automatic distress signal turned on. Besides I'm sure some bright individual on the rig has reported our kidnapping and the general direction that their craft set off to. Hell yeah, they're probably contacting the Navy right now." But Paul's thoughts were still on the weapon they had used to persuade them to come in the first place. Could even the Navy fight against such a thing?

CHAPTER EIGHT

R ecovering from the realization that these Atlantians could read minds, or at least Hellena could, Steve decided to press this issue of mind-reading with her, and to question her about it. "How did you know I was thinking that these Soschatch were slaves? Come on, tell me," Steve coaxed.

Hellena was silent for a moment, then turned to face her inquisitor and smiled. Placing her arm upon his shoulder, which had a soothing effect on him, she looked deep into his eyes as his mood began to mellow even more.

"Tell me," Steve implored. "Please?"

Hellena decided that they had reached an impasse with Steve's mind locked on that question. How could she find out anything more? Her father did tell her to discover all she could, in any way she could. She herself had told her girlfriends to be open with these strangers, so as to gain their confidence, and to find out what they could freely. She might as well answer him. It couldn't hurt at this stage of development, after all that was her father's orders, and this Steve already suspected the truth.

"Alright Steve, as you probably have guessed, I can read minds..."

Steve was ecstatic. His hunch was right, but this gave him little comfort. In fact it made him a bit more apprehensive. Although Hellena noted his apprehension, she continued, "...but not all of us can. Only the royal family and a few select members of the guard force have been given this ability. Oman, the one who controls destinies, has made it so."

Steve absent-mindedly thought, *Genetic engineering.*

"In a way it is genetic engineering, but very specialized and selective," Hellena interjected.

This whole conversation was getting a little unnerving for Steve. He was feeling like his privacy was being invaded.

Hellena could sense his uneasiness and suggested, "Perhaps you would feel better if I stayed out of your head, but you're going to have to help me. We need to know some things, and our time is running out."

"Ok, anything, what do you need to know?"

She told him. "We need to know the planet's status. Is the world still at war? Who rules the world, and from what continent? Will anyone come looking for you and the others, and what kind of weapons will they carry? What form of transportation is commonly in use on your world? What are the most deadly weapons your kind possesses?"

"Slow down, slow down. I have to take a moment to try to figure out how to answer all your questions, and I can't think straight and answer so many so quickly."

"I'm sorry, but this is very important. First off, do you think that there will be anyone searching for you in the next planet's orbit?"

"If you mean in the next twenty-four hours—yes. Our rig's crew was in contact with one of my countries warships that was patrolling south of our rig. We contacted it soon after we were hit by that wave your island's sudden surfacing caused. I'm sure that by now the remaining crew on the rig has reported to the ship that most of its crew was taken captive by your strange-looking submersible. If I know Mr. Holbrook, the whole episode was recorded by one of the rig's outside monitors. The ship is probably at the site by now, and its officers are viewing that recording. With this information they should be on their way here right about now. Next question."

"What do you think the people on that ship will do?"

"They'll probably send a search party using one of the ship's small landing boats, and they'll probably be armed."

"What kinds of weapons will they carry, how many of them do you expect the ship will send, and what other weapons will the ship have at its disposal?"

"Well, it's been a long time since I was in the service, but they'll probably send twelve to fifteen men carrying M-16s, M-14s, and an M-60 machine gun."

"What is machine gun? What kind of weapon is it? Is it anything like our maser?"

"You mean that thing that cut down one of the masts on the oil rig. No, it won't be anything like that. A machine gun is a device that fires projectiles made of lead. They are propelled at a rate that will cause the metal to penetrate flesh and damage or destroy organs in its path. The lead is propelled by a controlled explosion in a tube which it travels out of. That is a gun, and a machine gun is a gun that fires these lead projectiles at a very rapid rate."

"Lead? Explosion? What exactly do you mean? Wait a moment. I know I said I would stay out of your head, but if you'll just relax and think about this machine gun I'll be able to understand what you just told me."

"Ahhh, do you have to? That mind reading stuff gives me the creeps."

"You know it won't hurt, and besides if you concentrate on just that one thing I won't probe any deeper."

"Honest?"

"Honest. Trust me and just relax."

In another section of the island, Greg, Paul and Manny were following their escorts while the girls tried to interest them in a guided tour of the city. Paul was still mumbling something about how he'd like to get Tempest alone in a room for about five minutes. Greg and Manny were just awestruck by the different forms of architecture from different periods of time and places. All were massive structures and some of the more modern designs were made of a strange whitish stone similar to onyx.

Greg looked closer. *No, it looks more like slate only white. I've never seen stone quite like this before,* Greg contemplated, *and these building, some look like either ancient Greek or Roman, and others like the pyramids of Egypt and those of the Incas or Aztecs. Wow! I'm impressed.* "What do you think of these different styles of buildings?" Greg asked the two in general.

"They're really something," remarked Manny.

"They probably stole the plans from the Romans or someone," Paul chided.

"I don't know about that," Greg injected. "Perhaps they were the ones that gave the Romans and Egyptians the plans in the first place."

"Why do you keep defending these guys?" Paul demanded. "They take us captive, they demand answers to questions that could be dangerous to national security. I think they're a bunch of madmen and you want to hero worship them or defend their every action. What does it take for you to get pissed?"

"I don't like being here anymore than you do, but making waves ain't going to make it any easier. As for this hero-worshipping as you call it, I'm just impressed by all I've seen. If you weren't so damn bullheaded, you would be too. Look around you." Greg pointed toward a couple of buildings in the area, "This place shouldn't exist, but it does. And look at the different styles of buildings. History, my friend, history. They were there when these civilizations were growing up. Perhaps they influenced them. Perhaps they had something to do with the way civilization, as we know it, came about. I don't know, but even you have to be impressed with all this around us. This place *is* Atlantis."

"I'm impressed, but I don't like the way some of them talk down on us. And I wasn't too impressed with them cutting down one of the few antennas that weren't damaged by that wave. What do you think caused that anyway?"

"I don't know, but if this place wasn't here before and now it's here—if it came from the bottom of the ocean suddenly like a volcano erupting, this island's abrupt surfacing could have caused it."

"Yeah, I guess so. What now?" Paul still didn't sound impressed.

"Enjoy this tour, and just go with the flow," Greg said with encouragement. The three of them followed their beautiful escorts. They didn't see many other Atlantians along the way, and the ones they did passed them by without giving the strangers a second look. Greg thought it strange, but decided not to pursue it any further. Before too long, the escorts had led them to one of the Egyptian-styled buildings they had admired from a distance. One of the girls walked up to the open entrance and beckoned the others to follow.

"I don't know about this," Manny said nervously.

"Aw, come on. Where's your sense of adventure?" remarked Greg. "We're getting the chance of a lifetime to see things that no other outsiders have seen in thousands of years."

Manny mustered his courage and they all followed their escorts inside. It was very well illuminated, just like the great hall. Inside were gold statues, urns, and artifacts of a culture long since dead. The place reminded Greg of the Cairo museum in Egypt.

One of the escorts finally spoke, "Does this place look familiar to any of you?"

Greg could hardly contain himself, "Yes, it does, actually. A country we call Egypt. It is famous for its pyramids and lush history. Even the Romans were impressed when they conquered it."

"Oh, indeed. These Romans conquered Egypt. Do they still control Egypt?" asked one of their escorts.

"No, they don't," Greg answered. "Egypt now governs herself."

"What happened to the Romans?" inquired one of the other girls.

Visions of Cleopatra and Mark Anthony, and different movies he'd seen swirled through his head. In a fraction of a second his thoughts went deep into what he had learned in his history class, but still he drew a blank. "I don't know," was Greg's reply. "I must've slept through that class," he mused with a smile.

The trio walked about this chamber with its hieroglyphics on the wall and stone reliefs here and there. Some were layered with gold, while others were plain, like the ones Greg remembered seeing on one of his trips touring Egypt's Cairo museum.

The girls agreed that there was little more they could learn about the surface dwellers here, so they each took gentle hold of their companion's arm and guided them out of the pyramid-shaped building and onto an adjacent street. The men were eager to see what other sights their escorts would show them. Even Paul was beginning to relax. Walking through a maze of buildings, they came upon an oddly-shaped structure at the end of one of the roads. Here they were greeted by others of the captive crew, and while they compared notes on all they had seen, the girls grouped together to discuss their next destination.

Samantha spoke to the girls, "It is time for us to make our report to the council. We must take these men back to the citadel where they will find refreshments waiting for them."

"We have found very little out with our three," Greg's escort told them.

"It is of no matter, our time has ended. We will tell the council of everything we have heard and observed. They will know what to do next."

After a moment's silence, the girls dispersed and gathered their charges and invited them to follow them back to the citadel for a meal.

"Oh boy, eats!" Manny cried out.

"Let's go, I'm starving," announced Paul.

The men then followed their beautiful escorts back.

Gerald was the only one taken to the Atlantian's science center. His escort was Raval, one of the elite guard force. There he was taken to an amphitheater. Below him was another massive, bluish, glowing sphere, only this one pulsated with energy. "What is that thing?" he asked.

Raval answered, "That is Ular."

"What's an Ular?" Gerald persisted.

"Ular is that which contains all the stored knowledge acquired by our people throughout the ages. Ular is a brain and more. He has lived for two and a half millennia."

"Did you say, *lived?*" Gerald asked in amazement.

"Yes, I did. You use machines to think and to retain information, but what is more powerful, a machine or the brain that designed the machine?"

Gerald had to agree with the brain, but said, "A machine is faster and can do a task over and over without error, but I will agree that the brain is more powerful a tool when used properly. May I see this Ular?"

Raval thought that this would give him a chance to learn more about how advanced the surface dwellers science was, so he consented. "You may. Keep your eyes on the sphere, and be prepared to be amazed." Touching a control on a console near the object, Raval caused a change in the color of the pulsating blue sphere. First it turned an opaque white and then it began to become clear. Inside was a huge elongated transparent membrane floating in a lucent liquid. The inner weavings of a brain could be seen but there was more. The outer membrane pulsated and changed colors. Spots on it grew darker and larger then smaller and then clear again. Waves of dark stripes like ripples coursed from end to end. All this was happening in fractions of a second. Gerald was thoroughly astonished, he had never seen anything like this before. The only thing that he could possibly imagine that came close was what he had seen once in an aquarium, a cuttlefish, but this was so huge. No living creature known could have such a brain. How could this be?

"I said you would be amazed," Raval claimed with pride.

"How can you communicate with this brain?" asked Gerald.

"A select few of us were given the ability to communicate by thought. I am one such individual."

Gerald mused, *Then this would explain why Paul and the others threw down their weapons when he arrived.*

"That is correct," Raval replied.

Gerald about jumped out of his skin when he realized that Raval had been reading his thoughts.

"Try not to be alarmed. We wish you and your kind no harm. Our ability to communicate through telepathy was developed so we could become one with Ular. We do so to access information as needed. Ular's only requirement is that we let him see through our minds as we have done so now. He is all we are and much more."

"You mean to tell me my mind has been read by Ular as well?"

"Yes, Gerald."

"Frightening!"

"Only to the ignorant. Come, it is time to return to the citadel. There you will rejoin your friends." The sphere returned to its bright pulsating blue color when Raval removed his hand from the control. As they departed for the citadel, Raval took the lead with Gerald following, lost in his thoughts. Raval smiled, he had learned much about these surface dwellers.

Serena got up from the bed and went to a basin of water and washed her face. Tom leaned in her direction. "Now what?" he inquired.

"It is time you went to breakfast, and I must go before the council," she replied.

"Now?" Tom asked with a disappointed tone.

With a nod and a smile she softly cooed, "Now."

Tom got up, found his clothes and got dressed. Serena also got dressed, and walking to the doorway she said, "Come, I will show you the way to the dining hall."

Tom followed. Sex sure made a guy hungry. Boy, was he starved.

"Here you are." Serena pointed to the door.

"Will I see you again?" he asked.

"Possibly," Serena replied. Without saying another word, she turned and went down a different corridor.

Tom entered to find Bob and most of the others seated and already partaking of the fine spread before them.

"Come on, Tom. The food is great!" Bob said with his mouth full of some spiced meat.

Tom shrugged and went in to join them.

Although skeptical, Steve tried to relax. Anything to get this whole creepy thing over with.

"Come on, relax. It isn't creepy. It's a natural thing for me, like talking is for you. That's better, calm yourself and think about machine guns."

Almost hypnotically, Hellena's soft spoken words began to soothe Steve and he did begin to respond to her suggestions and thought about machine guns. Hellena was able to understand now what Steve was trying to explain to her. She then coaxed him into thinking about ships and weapons, transportation and communications and finally government and current events. This all took just a few minutes and she was very pleased that she was able to get all the information her father had desired. Upon receiving the last of the images from his mind, she bent down and gave him an affectionate kiss. This brought him out of his hypnotic haze. Gazing into his eyes, she asked, "Why is there no one nation in control? Why have a United Nations when they do nothing to end global hostilities, famine and sickness?"

All Steve could do was blink. First she knew nothing, and now she wanted to discuss world politics. Taking a moment to arrange his train of thought, he answered her inquiry, "To be honest, I don't know why the UN can't do more, but as to your question of why is there no one country in control, the world is full of different people, with different languages, beliefs and religions, with appointed leaders over them delegating the rules of each of their societies. There are just *too* many differences. Each country feels that their brand of government is the best, and when their ideals collide, fighting breaks out. I believe that the formula for true peace and unity is one of those unsolvable problems." Finding what he had just said humorous, he continued with a chuckle, "Not a bad recitation from a wildcatter."

"Wildcatter—What is a wildcatter?"

"Oh, I forgot. A wildcatter is a man who works on an oil rig, like me."

"Oh, I see, but how can you joke when your world is so bleak. There doesn't seem to be much hope with all this fighting."

"If that is all you got out of my head then you didn't get the whole picture. Life is what you make of it, no matter where you are from. Perhaps the world's politics are messed up, but there is love in the world and opportunity for those willing to work for it."

"So you feel there is no reason for despair, is that right?"

"Sure, I feel that way, don't you?"

"Yes, but what do you think will be the world's reaction once they discover our island has surfaced once again and that our civilization has survived?"

"I really don't know. Surprise most likely, I guess, but maybe anger at first because your people kidnapped us!"

"What choice had we?" Helena said defensively. "Tell me you would have done something different if it were your people isolated at the bottom of an ocean, then suddenly finding yourselves surfaced and in a strange new world."

Steve said nothing. He knew that she was right and sympathized with her situation, but what could he do, he was a prisoner. He then answered her, "No, I'd have probably done the same thing, but like you said, time is short. Did you find out everything you needed to know?"

"Yes I did, thank you. See, it didn't hurt," she said, giggling as she remembered his earlier uneasiness.

When Steve had finished his sandwich and juice they departed. It was time to return, so Hellena took his hand and led them back to the citadel. Along the way she said, "Just in case you are still hungry, a small feast has been prepared for you and your compatriots. I must report to the Council of Elders, as well as my girlfriends. You and the others will be left alone in the dining area for a short time while the council meets. There you will be able to tell each other of your experiences here freely and in privacy. We have nothing to hide from you, and I am sure that the council will order your return to the structure from which you came very soon. You may assure your friends of that."

They walked the wide, gentle upward-sloping streets of the city toward their final destination. The tall massive doors began to open as they approached. Once inside the chamber, Steve was lost. Hellena had no problem navigating her way through the maze of corridors till she had brought Steve to the dining area. She stopped just before the entrance and turned to face him. "I want to thank you for your cooperation, understanding, and help."

Steve remained silent at first, but took this moment to put his arms around her waist and drew her closer to himself. He gave her a passionate kiss. "I hope that I will get a chance to see you again sometime."

Without even blinking she replied, "I hope so too, but I really must be going. Your friends are already inside and I can sense the council's impatience. I must go now." Slipping out of his embrace she turned and hurried to the council chamber.

When Steve entered the dining area he saw the rest of the captive crew sitting at a table eating their fill and talking about all they had seen. Spotting Steve's entrance, Tom motioned him to come to the table. As he approached, he heard Paul say, " ...and then this Tempest guy asked about the weapons we have. I didn't know what to tell him, but after seeing what their little toy did to one of the masts I decided that ours had better be better, so I mixed telling them about the Star Wars project that the U.S. is working on with that of the movie and what I've read from some sci-fi books." Paul chuckled, "I really got his goat, then him and the others left in a huff. What about you guys? Did you tell them anything?"

Steve just sat down. He didn't say a word; of course he wouldn't admit that he'd allowed Hellena to pick his brain. By now she was surely reporting to the council.

One of the other men spoke up and said, "Naw, me, Jack, and Don just walked around the city with three of the best-looking babes we've ever seen. We didn't talk much, but I'll tell you I sure was impressed with everything I saw."

Steve smiled grimly as he thought, *They just probably read their minds too.*

Paul shifted to face a very quiet Steve. "Hell, we haven't heard you say much of anything, and you came back last. Did they get anything from you?"

Steve didn't know how to answer. How would these guys react if he told them that he freely answered all of Hellena's questions? They didn't even know that the Atlantians can read thoughts. Deciding he had better tell them all he knew and what he had told Hellena, he replied, "I didn't tell them anything, but I didn't have to. They can read minds and my guess is that you all gave them information without knowing it."

"What makes you say that?" Paul interrupted.

"While I was touring the city I saw these very tall, strong-looking men picking up large slabs of stone. Some of them were clearing out the rubble while the others were repairing and reconstructing the buildings. I asked my escort about them, and she said that it was their work. I thought they were being treated like slaves; the operative word being *thought*. I was just thinking that they were slaves and my escort got all bent out of shape and argued with me defensively. Then I pressed the issue that I had only *thought* about their status as slaves. Eventually she admitted that she and some of the others can actually read minds. I wouldn't be a bit surprised if all our escorts could pick our brains."

As what Steve had just told them sank in, everyone became very quiet. A silence fell across the room. Paul broke the silence roaring, "Man, you mean to tell me that all these guys here can read minds? *Shit*, come on!"

Steve answered, "I didn't say everyone, but my escort, the council, and probably the other escorts can as well. Right now they're reporting what they found out to their leaders."

"Dammit!" Paul spat. "Then they know what I told them was a pack of fuckin' lies." Pausing a moment, he leaned toward Steve and demanded, "What did *you* tell them?"

"As I said before, I didn't have to say anything. She read my mind and found the truth," Steve stated flatly. "That there was probably a ship coming to rescue us, what kind of weapons it has, and the political state of the world."

Paul gritted his teeth, grumbled, "That's fine, man. Now they'll capture the rescue ship and we'll never get off this damn fuckin' rock!"

"Oh, shut up!" Steve exclaimed with defiance toward Paul, who was stunned into silence by his sudden forceful outburst. "That argument you had with one of their leaders was most likely staged in order to get your mind focused on the information they needed. You're so thick-headed that they used your own arrogance against you. You gave them everything they wanted all by yourself." His last statement reeked of smugness.

Paul glared, his temper flaring as he pounded his clinched fist onto the table before reaching across at Steve in an attempt to strike him. Before he could make contact, Bob stood up and pushed him back into his chair.

"Sit down! Both of you!" Bob shouted. "Fighting amongst ourselves isn't going to solve anything!"

Paul sat and slowly started to cool off. Steve sat down as well.

"You mean to tell me they can really read our minds?" asked one of the crewmen seated near the end of the table.

"That's what he's been telling us, stupid!" blazed the man sitting next to him while giving him a slap across the back of his head with an open hand.

"You're telling me that when I was thinking how much I'd like to climb that girl's long legs and get up in her fine lookin' bod, she knew exactly what I was thinking?" blurted out another. "Damn, if I knew that I would've really fantasized."

Everyone around him laughed, except Gerald, who just shook his head from side to side. He didn't truly know these guys. They were just too much. He couldn't believe what he was hearing. They were animals.

"Alright, we know that they can read minds and that they possess a very powerful weapon," Tom stated calmly. "They now know our capabilities and that a rescue ship will be here soon. They appear to have all the answers they wanted when we arrived. They haven't hurt us, and I think they would have by now if that was their intention. After all, they have what they want." Addressing Steve, he asked, "Did your escort say anything about if or when they might take us back to the rig?"

"She only said that she was sure that the council would let us return soon."

"And you trust her?" Paul snapped.

"Yes, I do," Steve replied matter-of-factly.

"Alright, you two!" Bob shouted. "Enough bickering between yourselves. We need to make a plan of escape in case they try to keep us any longer."

Manny whined, "What can we do? They can read our minds. What plans can we make that they won't find out about?"

"Good point! Any suggestions?" Bob inquired.

"I don't have any suggestions, just one question. How would we leave if we could escape? The only sort of craft I've seen was that blue bubble thing, and I saw no way to control it," Tom stated.

Steve mused, "Perhaps it also is mind-controlled."

In another part of the citadel, the council had gathered to hear the report from the newcomers' escort. Serena had just finished her report and now it was Hellena's turn. Atar's daughter went to the control console on the table and placed a hand on one of the crystals. In an instant the four back panels glowed brilliantly and an image of a warship came into view, followed by a series of images representing the various weapons she had learned about from Steve. "A ship like this one will most likely come toward our island searching for the surface dwellers. These are the types of weapons it may carry." Once more images came into view. Violent images from Steve's memories of the Gulf wars. "This is some of the savagery we may have to contend with. His people and many places around the world are actively engaged in battles as I speak." More images came into focus. These were of the U.S. President, the different countries of the world and the UN. "This is Steve's leader," she continued, "the various governments in power to date, and a place where each government's representative meet to discuss world affairs. This may be the place to confer with the other nations of the world on our form of government and what we as a people have to offer the surface dwellers and the possibility of establishing trade."

Before she proceeded further, Atar added, "My daughter is right. We should decide our role in man's history. As in the past our ancestors influenced many nations, offering advice and scientific information. There is much we could do to uplift their society. We could exchange knowledge and offer our proficiency in the life sciences, providing cures for most of the world's maladies."

Marrick interrupted Atar, "I say No! Why offer any exchange of information when we hold the greatest storehouse of wisdom throughout the ages? The surface dwellers we have observed have demonstrated that most of the knowledge we once shared was either lost or wasted. In the time our ancestors flourished, there was fear for our studies and fear begets senseless violence. What about now? These surface dwellers cannot accept that which they cannot comprehend and this may lead to violence directed at our people for little more than the fact that we have survived. We know by the reports of the escorts and our own meeting with the surface dwellers that we are superior to them in many ways. They do not possess weapons as powerful as our own. We could reach out and take control of this world and then guide it, through our rule, toward a more stable civilization."

Atar refuted Marrick. "By attempting to take control of the world by force you would have us degenerate to their barbaric level. I say no! We are more civilized than that. Through our influence we can uplift these people and guide them to their Utopia. As our ancestors tried before to better mankind physically, we can also better him intellectually and so improve their society. It is conceivable that we can instill a lasting peace throughout the world. Humans must learn to work with humans."

The rest of the council nodded in approval at Atar's wisdom, and Marrick sat down persuaded that Atar was right. Without hesitation, Hellena once more placed her hand on the controls. This time the transposed images of ships, cars, trains, planes, jets, rockets, and other forms of transportation. "These are the various vehicles the surface dwellers use to travel. The power of flight is no longer a physical limitation, but by the use of machines they can fly."

Tempest spoke up, "As I surmised, these surface dwellers use crude and limited mechanisms to travel. They hurl themselves into the void of space to what end?"

"I don't know," Hellena replied, "but their machines can fly and move very fast."

"The use of these devices is unnatural," Tempest injected. "If humanity were meant to fly we would have wings. We have adapted our humans to a watery environment, now we can adapt them to the sky. We need no such contrivances."

Atar interrupted, "We may not need such machines, but they do possess a technology which we know little about." Atar pointed to the images on the wall. I say we should decide to communicate with these surface dwellers' leaders and arrange an exchange of cultural information. We have been isolated for so long, yet each civilization, theirs and ours, could benefit from such an exchange of ideas. Perhaps together we could obtain the goal our forefathers had in mind and create the perfectly adapted human. Only time will tell. We also know that we need not fear these people, for in fact we have greater power at our disposal. We are stronger physically and I believe much more intelligent."

Hellena added, "As I was obtaining this information, the surface dweller I was with discovered my telepathic ability. For that I am sorry, but after his initial shock wore off I was able to probe his mind and acquire these facts. I also discovered that these people are limited to using speech for communication. By now he has passed this information on to the other newcomers. What should be done now that they know of our telepathic abilities?"

"You said that your charge was shocked by this discovery?" Tempest inquired. "If this is so, how too will the entirety of this planet react to such knowledge? With shock, mistrust, envy? Whatever their reaction, it may be dangerous for us. What humanity does not understand, it destroys! The unknown can frighten and overwhelm."

"Are you such an authority on mankind?" Hellena spoke up in defense. "We only have our memories of the past and what little we have gleaned in this short span of time from these surface dwellers. We cannot base an entire planet on these few individuals or their memories."

Tempest argued, "Why not? There is enough diversity in this sampling of humankind to draw such a conclusion."

"Then factor this into your hypothesis. The one I was with, Steve, has a kind soul. I know because I touched it. While I was showing him the city he discovered my telepathic ability. At first he was uneasy, but it wasn't long before he took this all in stride. When I told him about what information we needed, he willingly allowed me to read his mind. He went so far as to focus his attention on each matter, providing me with the clear images I've shown you. Does that sound like a people who will learn to fear and loath us? I don't think so."

"He may be the exception to the rule," Tempest protested.

Atar placed a comforting hand on his daughter's shoulder and caused her to take her seat. Everyone was quiet. Atar had come to a decision. "Tempest is right, my dear. Mankind fears the unexplainable."

"But what about Steve? Surely his actions disprove that conjecture," Hellena countered.

"Steve may very well be everything you claim him to be, but I feel he is only the exception to the rule. We have come a long way since our forefathers used fear to protect this island while attempting to reshape humanity, but I am afraid after what we have witnessed, mankind is still in its infancy."

Addressing everyone present, Atar continued with great conviction. "There is a warship approaching our island, our home. We could destroy it or take it captive, but that would only serve to fan the flames of hate and suspicion among mankind. It is possible my daughter's feeling in this matter is correct, and we have nothing to be concerned about regarding these surface dwellers, but we must do what is best for our people. If I am to make a mistake, I would rather err on the side of caution. Therefore we cannot allow the surface dwellers to feel that we are a threat or any different than they are. We must erase all knowledge of our telepathic abilities from the minds of our guests and take great caution in our future dealings with them and their kind not to let them become aware of any of our physical improvements—at least not until we are certain of their ability to accept these differences."

Nodding to the council as a signal for unification, for a moment the council became one mind. "Then it is agreed. You all know what we must do. Marrick, you and Hellena go and inform our people of the council's decree," Atar directed. With a slight bow toward Atar and the council, Marrick and Hellena departed the great hall.

Turning to Sara, one of Hellena's girlfriends who earlier had given her report, Atar gave her an order, "Go and bring our guests before the council. We have reached a decision."

Bowing ever so slightly to Atar and the elders, she turned and departed for the dining hall. As she entered, the buzzing of conversation between the men and the clatter of utensils while they ate suddenly became silent. Every eye turned in the direction of this long, dark-haired nymph who just entered the room. She was drop-dead gorgeous. After taking a few more steps into the room, she stopped. The crew's eyes locked onto every gentle sway of her body as if they were starving and she was a meal to devour. Now that she knew she had their attention, she began to talk to them from across the room, "Excuse me for interrupting your meal, but the council wishes to meet with all of you at this moment."

Tom was still amazed at how clear the acoustics were in this room. She was so far away, yet she sounded like she was standing right next to him.

"Alright," said Tom. "We were hoping to meet with them soon ourselves." Turning to the slack-jawed crew he stated, "Come on, you guys, stop gaping and let's go see what the council wants. Maybe it's news about our release."

"Fat chance," remarked Paul. The tall black man remained skeptical. "They have something up their sleeve and I'd give my left nut to find out what it is."

Steve frowned and just hoped no one was probing Paul's head.

The men pulled away from the table and walked toward Sara. At the same time four servant girls resembling the same four as the previous night worked at clearing the table.

Sara led them down the hall to a doorway already opened, with two guards on either side of the massive stone portals. As they entered they saw before them the council seated along the back wall. Behind them and all around every wall panel, ceiling section and floor tile glowed the same eerie bluish color of the submersible that had brought them there. When the last man had entered, the guards pulled the massive stone doors shut behind them and they also turned the same bluish tint as the rest of the room.

"Welcome," Atar announced. "Please do not be alarmed by the change in the lighting. We Atlantians, as you wish to call us, prefer this light to the harsher hues. We find that it makes for a more serene environment."

Bob, the unwilling leader of the group spoke up, "That's well and good, but we believe you have something of importance to tell us. Is it about us returning to our rig?"

Without hesitation Atar addressed the question. "As you are probably aware, one of your warships is en route to our island. We were going to return you at this time, but we feel that we had better assure your warship of your safety and our intentions first. We do not wish to do battle with anyone. Our only desire is to remain in peace and perchance arrange an exchange of cultural information and scientific knowledge. Therefore, you are invited to enjoy our hospitality until which time the warship arrives."

"You are keeping us fuckin' hostage to prevent retaliation for kidnapping us in the first place. You're afraid that the ship out there will reduce your island to rubble!" Paul shouted vehemently.

Before anyone could attempt to calm Paul down, Atar responded to his outburst. "You are partly correct, surface dweller. Your kind are too quick to react as you have just demonstrated. We wish to avoid any such conflict, but I assure you it is not fear that prompts us to this decision." Placing a hand on one of the controls near his seat, he caused the center panel behind him to change color and an image of an ancient Greek warship came into view. "In our very distant past we learned to use the sun's power as a weapon. Surely you have heard of this. Look and see what just a focused mirror of sunlight can do." The image began to move. The ship came toward a rocky coastal scene when suddenly a beam of light hit the wooden vessel and it burst into flames. "How much more powerful are our masers? As you can see, it is not fear for ourselves. We just do not wish to destroy anything senselessly." Atar removed his hand and the panel returned to its original eerie bluish hue. "We now have our answers and have chosen a course of action. When your ship arrives for you, we will let you go with them, but first we will have its captain arrange for an audience at your United Nations with the leaders of the world. Our presence is no longer a secret and the whole world should be informed of our existence and what we have to offer in trade."

With all due humility, Tom replied, "We understand..."

"Do you?" Tempest cut him off in mid-sentence. "Do you really? I don't think so, but you shall." Upon saying that, the room became very silent. All the councilmen's heads were bowed toward the gathered men. The walls, ceiling, and floor's color began to glow an even brighter blue, pulsated once, then returned to the normal whitish color as when the group was first brought to this chamber.

Atar rose from his seat and calmly said, "Welcome. My name is Atar and we are the council of Atlantis...."

CHAPTER NINE

"USS *Lavan* to *Skyoil-One*, do you copy?"

"USS *Lavan* this is *Skyoil-One*, we copy."

"This is Commander Wells, is Mr. Holbrook there?"

"Wait one." The communication technician called out across the control room, "Mr. Holbrook, I have Commander Wells from the *USS Lavan* on channel two. He wishes to speak to you."

David stood up from the derrick's construction plans on the center table, "Alright, go ahead and cut down masts seven and nine, as long as you are sure you can use their parts to repair six," David explained to Jenkins, the man with him at the table. He then turned and raced to the mike Corey was holding out for him. "Holbrook here."

"Mr. Holbrook, this is Commander Wells. I just wanted to inform you that our lookout has spotted your rig and we should be alongside in about forty-five minutes. Do you have anything more to report?"

"Not at this time. No changes since our men were taken aboard that strange bubble-looking thing. If you'll wait a moment I'll check again with *our* lookout." Putting the mike in his left hand, David pointed to the small hand radio on the plotting table. "Jack, hand me the radio." Jack picked up the radio and passed it to David. "John, anything new since your last report?"

"No, Mr. Holbrook," John replied recognizing David's voice. "Nothing since that blue glow faded as it approached that new island in the distance. I haven't seen anything else."

"OK, thanks, I'll send your relief up shortly."

"That would be nice, I'm a bit bushed," John said.

Putting down the radio and returning the mike to his right hand,

David continued, "Commander Wells, I've just talked with our look-out and he has nothing more to report."

"Thank you, that coincides with our sonar readings. Our lookout announced spotting that new island. I'm anxious to look at that re-cording you made of the whole incident."

"I'll have it ready for viewing by your arrival, *Skyoil-One* out. Corey, get the recording ready," David ordered as he gave him back the mike. "Jack, relieve John on lookout. I'm going into my office and take a catnap. Lord knows there isn't any more I can do." Saying that, David headed out of the control room. As he got to the door he said, "Wake me up when the *Lavan* has finished tying up," and then he was gone.

Forty-five minutes later the *Lavan* approached the rig. As the ship maneuvered into one of the tanker berths, Jack climbed down from his lookout station to meet with Jenkins and with John, who had just enough time to finish his breakfast and wash his face. "I'll sure be glad when this is all over. Do you think our people are alright?" Jenkins asked John as they approached the berth.

"You saw what they did to the mast. If they wanted them dead they would have done it then," John remarked with reassurance. "I'm sure they're alright. We just have to get them back, that's all."

"Alright you two, let's help the ship with its lines," Jack said as he caught up with the others.

With only the three of them to assist, it took nearly twenty min-utes for the ship to be fully moored. With that done, Jenkins gave the ship's crew a hand with the refueling hoses. He couldn't help too much as he was one of the few remaining workers on the rig, and there was much work needing his attention.

Jack came aboard to escort the captain to the control room while John went on ahead to wake Mr. Holbrook. Shaking the captain's hand he stated, "Welcome, captain, am I glad to see you. This place has been a nut-house since that wave hit and our crew was taken captive. I sure hope you can help."

The captain replied, "I hope so too, but first I want to see that tape of the incident."

"Yeah, sure," mumbled Jack. "Follow me." He continued down the passageway without looking back. With the captain following, Jack returned to the control room.

John made his way to David's office just minutes ahead of Jack and the commander. John knocked on the office door, then walked in. "Excuse me, sir, the captain of the *Lavan* is on his way with Jack. They are moored in berth two and are taking on fuel."

"Is the recording ready for viewing?" David asked.

"I don't know, I came here straight away to make sure you were up before the captain arrived."

Sitting up on the couch, David rubbed the sleep from his eyes and then stretched. "Thank you," David replied. "Go tell Corey to get the recording ready. I'm sure the captain will want to see it right away."

Without a further word, John turned and walked out. A minute after David had a chance to run a comb through his hair there was a knock on the door. "Come in," he barked. Jack and the captain walked in.

"Welcome and thanks for coming. We sure can use some help," David stated as he offered the commander his hand.

Shaking hands, the captain responded, "Thank you. Is the video ready? I would like to see what we're up against."

"I believe it is. If you will just follow me to the control room, we can view it there." The three of them departed the office with David directing them to the control room.

Clapping his hands together the captain said, "Quickly, we've got to get this show on the road."

"Over here," called out Corey, pointing to his monitor screen. He wasn't at all impressed with the captain's remark about this being a show. People's lives were at stake. When the group had gathered around the console and all eyes toward the monitor, Corey pressed a button and the video began to replay the previous night's incident. The captain's mouth fell open as the blue bubble approached the rig, surfaced and then opened up.

"What the hell is that thing?" he said as he saw a mast being cut down in seconds.

"I wish I knew what they were saying," Jack commented as he watched the silent conversation between Raval and Bob.

"They just walked aboard like sheep," remarked the captain.

"Our guess is that the cutting down of the mast was a threat to get them to go on board the strange craft," David commented.

"Burn me a copy of this recording so I can show it to my officers. We will then be able to better determine what course of action would be best to take," assured the commander.

"Sure thing," said David as he indicated to Corey to give the captain a DVD. "Just let us know what you decide."

"I'll do that," the captain replied, heading for the door.

"I'll show you the way out," Jack said as the two of them left the control room for the ship.

"What now?" asked Corey, looking at David.

"Wait and see," he replied. "I sure hope the men are safe." His thoughts drifted to the new island.

The captain and Jack walked toward the petty officer of the watch, who stood at attention. He saluted the captain. "Good morning, sir."

Returning the salute he replied, "Good morning, Petty Officer Smith, log this man aboard and I will escort him to the wardroom. Officer of the Deck, pass the word to have all the ship's officers meet me in the wardroom at this time."

"Aye sir," he said and repeated the order.

"Messenger of the watch, pass the word on the I-MC, all ship's officers your presence is requested in the wardroom," the OOD ordered.

"Aye, aye sir," replied the messenger of the watch and repeated the OOD's order verbatim back to him and then again on the I-MC.

As he followed the captain to a spacious room, Jack thought to himself, *And they say civilian bureaucracy has a lot of red tape, ssshheeee!* Some of the officers were already there while others trickled in soon thereafter. A total of twenty-five came and sat down at the wardroom's table and commenced talking nervously among themselves until the captain began to speak. Everyone became silent as the captain directed the petty officer standing at the rear of the room, "Steward, turn on the TV and put this DVD in the player—after it starts, leave." The steward took the DVD and did as he was instructed. With that, all eyes focused on the TV.

Though Jack had grown accustomed to the scene they were viewing, it had the same sickening effect on him as when he had first observed the abduction. One of the officers called out, "What the hell is that?" when the view from the monitor hit the blue surfacing object.

The captain told him, "Just watch." After it was finished he had the equipment switched off, and asked, "Any ideas on how we should go about rescuing these men?"

One officer offered, "We should send the helo over the island and take some pictures, determine the best place to send in a landing party or recon team."

The commander mulled this over for a moment then said in agreement, "That sounds like a good plan of action for now. Perhaps we could drop a search party of four or five men, if a reasonable spot can be found. Any further suggestions?" There was no reply, so he added, "Any comments?"

This time an ensign seated at the far end spoke up. "What did they use to cut down that mast? I saw no visible weapon. For that matter, why didn't these men run for cover? Why did they just walk on board like a bunch of sheep?"

Jack answered these questions. "We don't know exactly what type of weapon it was. We saw no light, but feel that it must have been some type of laser. The piece still attached to the rig looked as if it had melted like a candle. As for why they didn't take cover, and why they just walked on board, we speculate that the conversation between our site foreman and the alien on that strange craft was a threat toward the men on the rig. Blasting away our antenna was their method of persuasion. Possible shock or a feeling that they were in some way protecting the rest of us on the rig caused them to decide to board that strange craft. In any case we need your help to get them back safely." Jack sat down. He was exhausted for having been up the entire previous night.

Wells directed his next command to the communications officer, "Send a message out to Commander, Atlantic Fleet and inform him of our present position, the situation here, and how we plan to deal with it. Send this out on the classified channel."

The communications officer rose. "Aye sir." He then departed the wardroom and went to the radio room located on the 0-2 deck level.

He pointed to a pair of officers. "You two get the helo ready and organize a team of four men to accompany you in case you have an opportunity to drop off a search party." Looking at his watch the captain added, "It is now zero-nine-thirty. I want everyone to be ready for departure by eleven-hundred hours."

The two officers simultaneously replied, "Aye, aye sir," then got up from the table and left to carry out the commander's orders.

Turning to Jack, the captain stated, "I'll have one of the officers escort you off the ship. Tell Mr. Holbrook that I want to hold onto this recording a little longer, and tell him what we have decided to do about his men. After we get a better picture of what we are up against I'll send in a rescue party and get your men back, but be certain you do not use your radio to inform anyone. We must have restricted communications about this until it is over. We don't want to tip our hand before we get a chance to play it." After gesturing to the executive officer to escort Jack off the ship, he dismissed the others. Time could be critical. "Steward, some coffee!" he shouted. The situation was getting to him as well.

Jack returned to the control room where he found David and Corey and made his report.

"Well, at least that's something," said David. "I guess we'll just have to wait and see." Turning to face Jack, he suggested, "Jack, I've told John to go get some sleep. How about you relieving Corey at the console so he and I can get in a two-hour nap? At that time have Jenkins wake us up, and then you and he can get some sleep. I know you're tired. We all are, but you've had the most amount of sleep in the past forty-eight hours."

Jack simply replied, "Alright," and walked over to the console where Corey explained the set up to him.

"I've placed everything on full automatic. The server is controlling the works. If you get bored you can flip on the outside monitors and look around, or put them in scan mode and watch each sequence about one minute," pointing to the monitor's controls above the large screen in the center of the console.

Jack shook his head. *And these guys get $105,000 for this. I'm in the wrong business*, reflected Jack before saying, "Yeah, I got it. Get some sleep and I'll wake you in about two hours."

"Thanks," said Corey and went to his stateroom for some much-needed rest. David had already gone, which left Jack all alone in the control room.

Sitting down in front of the main metering console, he flipped on monitor four. It was the one that had recorded the events of the previous night's episode. As he peered at the monitor Jack noticed only how quiet and lonely it looked outside. He should have brought a book to read. He then flipped the switch on the monitor panel to scan. The time seemed to drag on. The control room remained dead quiet. No word from the ship—nothing.

After Jenkins finished refueling the ship he wandered up to the control center. There was nothing more for him to do. The ship had taken over the lookout duties. Stopping at the recreation room along the way, he picked up a deck of cards, and arriving at the control room he asked Jack, "We've got about forty-five minutes to kill before it's time to wake the others. Do you want to play some cards?"

"Sure, what kind?" returned Jack.

"How about spades?"

"Spades? That's a four handed game!"

"Not the way I play it." He gave Jack a wink. "All you have to do is look at the top card. If you like it—keep it, if not, throw it away and keep the next. You either keep or throw the second card depending on what you do with the first, but once you decide you can't change your mind. Then we play like usual. Minimum bid is five. Any questions?"

Jack shook his head and said, "No."

"Good," said Jenkins shuffling the deck, "Cut?"

Jack just waved his hand over the deck, so Jenkins took the cards and placed them down in front of him. Jack then proceeded to take his hand. This went on for the next fifteen minutes.

With a roar and a rumble the helicopter on the *Lavan* took off. "What's that?" asked Jenkins.

"The *Lavan's* helo," remarked Jack, unconcerned. "They're going on a recon of the island."

"Shouldn't we inform the others?" asked Jenkins.

"Nope," remarked Jack, "they already know. Besides, it's out of our hands now. Let's get back to the cards," he suggested. When the alarm sounded on Jack's watch they ended the game with a score of 1,673 to 1,408 in Jack's favor.

"Since I won, why don't you go wake the others up?" suggested Jack.

Jenkins didn't need to be told twice. His bed was calling him and he sure was tired. He left to wake up the others: David first, then Corey, and then John. After waking John he told him that he was going straight to bed and did so without delay. The others met in the control room.

"Any word from the *Lavan?*" David asked Jack.

"None."

Sliding into the seat next to Jack, Corey said, "I'll take over—any problems?" he inquired as his eyes did a once-over of the familiar console.

"No problems and thanks," responded Jack.

As he left, David told Jack, "We'll get you guys in six hours provided you're not needed sooner." Jack just put his hand up in the air and waved backwards as he went out the door. He could care less. All he wanted was some sleep.

"Rainbow-One to *Lavan*, com-check," came the word from the helicopter as it departed.

"Rainbow-One, aye we copy. CIC has you on their scopes and tracking," replied the *Lavan*.

"Rainbow-One, aye copy. Proceeding one-six-niner magnetic on direct course for the island."

"*Lavan*, aye copy. Ending transmission until next com-check. Your fifteen minute mark—ready—mark!"

"Mark, aye. My fifteen minute next com-check. Rainbow-One, out."

There was tense silence for the next interval—then came the familiar, "Rainbow-One to *Lavan*, com-check."

"Com-check, aye. What do you have to report?"

"Aye, wait one—approaching island's northern side. There appears to be three concentric circles, probably coral reefs encompassing the island. Passing over the mountain ridge now," said the pilot as he made his way over the island.

Suddenly the weapons officer shouted, "Look at that!" as he pointed toward the larger peak they just flew over.

"Come in, Rainbow-One. What have you spotted?" came the request from the *Lavan's* communication officer.

"Rainbow-One to *Lavan*, the weapons officer has spotted a live volcano within the island's largest peak. I am continuing to take pictures and am now passing over a large dome-shaped rock formation. There appears to be no sign of life down there. No vegetation, only rock. I can see no cave or entry point into the island. Making a second pass now."

"*Lavan*, aye copy." There was no more word for a moment, then came Rainbow-One again. "*Lavan*, we have located a flat spot on the island's southwest side. I am setting down to drop off search party at this time. Their next com-check on my fifteen minute mark—mark! Returning to ship with video, over."

"*Lavan*, aye. Understand. Out."

Another long, tense fifteen minutes went by when the helicopter approached and made its landing, but there was no word from the search party. After landing, the pilot made his way directly to the com shack where the captain, communication officer and three others were chomping at the bit waiting for the search party to call in. As he entered he heard the CO say, "Damn it, check in!"

"Haven't they checked in yet?" asked the pilot.

"No," remarked the coms officer, "and they are six minutes past due."

"You had better prep the helo. You may have to fly back up to search and rescue them," suggested the captain.

"Yes sir," replied the XO before departing.

"Sparks, send a message to Com-Lant-Fleet and appraise him of our situation and course of action taken. No special channel."

"Aye," was the officer's only reply as he busied himself with the transmitter.

"I'm going to grab a bite to eat and then go to the bridge," said the captain.

"Now set the special sea and anchor detail," the OOD announced over the 1-MC.

The messenger made his way through the maze of ladders and passageways to the derrick's control room. He quickly told those present of the ship's preparations for getting underway and requested their assistance with the lines.

"Why, what's going on?" asked David.

The messenger glanced down at the floor and then back before explaining, "We have lost contact with our search party and the captain has decided to take the ship closer to the island."

David told the messenger that they would be right with him. "Corey, you stay here and mind the store. John and I will help the ship with their lines. No sense waking the others. I doubt you could if you wanted to." On his way out the door he said, "Come on John, get the lead out, let's get going." Departing the control room and leaving Corey all alone, the two soon caught up with the messenger, who was still trying to navigate his way out of the derrick. "Follow me, lad," David said as the two passed him in the corridor.

By the time they arrived, the ship's special sea and anchor detail was fully assembled. Four men readied the brow to take it on board. As they approached David turned to John. "You help them with the lines and I'm going on board and see if I can hitch a ride with them. They're our men out there too, and this just sit-back-and-wait crap is driving me crazy."

"I understand," came the sympathetic reply from John. "If you go with the ship keep us informed."

"I will," he promised as he crossed the brow.

The OOD came up to him and said, "Sir, you must leave the ship. Can't you see we are about to get underway?"

David ignored him and just said, "I'm David Holbrook. It is most urgent that I speak to your captain."

The OOD didn't really know what to do, so he called the bridge and requested to speak with the commander. "Captain, I have a man by the name of David Holbrook here. He says that it is most urgent that he speak with you."

"Very well, put him on," answered the captain. The OOD handed David the phone.

"Hello," said David.

"What's so important? Can't you see we're getting underway?" the captain retorted sharply.

"I know you're getting underway. That's just it. I want to go with you," came the plaintive plea from David. "Those are my men out there too, and I just can't sit back, wait and do nothing," David explained.

"You know we can't take civilians on board," the captain rebutted.

"I know the Navy has taken PACE instructors on board, and they're civilians," David said.

"We don't know what we may encounter. I can't take the responsibility for you in case you get hurt," explained the captain, hoping this would persuade him to give up his notion of going with the ship.

"I'll take the responsibility myself; let me go with you. I may be of some help. I know my men."

After a long pause, the commander reluctantly replied, "Alright then, you can come along, but you must do as you're told."

"Thank you sir, I will."

"Let me talk to the OOD."

"Here, he wants to talk to you." David handed the phone to the duty officer.

"Yes sir," answered the OOD as he placed the phone to his ear.

"Log Mr. Holbrook aboard. List him as an official observer then shift the watch to the bridge," came the captain's order.

"Yes sir." He hung up the phone. "I don't know why he let you come aboard, but come over here." He pointed to the watch stand. "I need to log you aboard." Turning to the petty officer of the watch he instructed, "Pass the word over the 1-MC, the Officer of the Deck is shifting his watch from the starboard quarterdeck to the bridge."

"Aye, sir." The watch repeated the order then again over the 1-MC.

By this time David had been logged in. He shouted across the brow to John, "I'm going with them. Take care of my rig." He followed the messenger up to the bridge.

The bridge was a beehive of activity with all the preparations. The brow was already placed on board and stowed. Then came the word over the 1-MC to single up all lines. The process of getting underway was running smoothly.

Commander Wells continued giving orders until the ship was well away from the rig. He then gave the steering order and heading, which placed them in direct route to the mysterious, foreboding island. Before relinquishing command to the OOD he had the order passed to secure the special sea and anchor detail.

Afterwards, the commander took the mike of the 1-MC and made an announcement to his crew. "This is the captain speaking. You are all probably wondering why we have changed course for an oil rig in the middle of the Atlantic and now are abruptly getting underway again. Last night, we received an urgent request for assistance from *Skyoil-One*. A tidal wave had caused them a lot of damage. Soon afterwards, we received another message. Fourteen of its men were taken captive by a strange vessel that surfaced near the rig. Earlier today, we sent out one of our helos to take pictures of an island we believe the captors came from. We also dropped off a small search party. That team has failed to report in. We have no idea what has happened to them. We can only speculate that they may have been captured. We are presently on course for that island and I intend to do everything in our power to rescue these men. We may have to use force, so the expertise that some of us demonstrated when we were off the coast of Syria may have to be utilized again. We must be ready for anything. I just thought you should be informed of our action. Com-Lant-Fleet has also been informed. That is all." David could hear cheers resounding all over the destroyer. The captain had the word passed to set the battle-ready watch throughout the ship.

"Now set the condition three watch, section two," was the next announcement over the 1-MC. Men were scurrying everywhere before final reports came in from all stations that they were manned and ready.

After all the excitement of getting underway and setting the condition three watch was over, David heard a dull, chiming sound playing a tune similar to what he'd heard at a racetrack. He asked one of the petty officers, "What is that all about?"

The crewman replied, "Mess call for the officers."

"Let's eat," suggested the captain. David followed him to the wardroom where a virtual feast was set before them.

The captured sailors were disarmed and brought before the council. The rig's crew had already been dispersed and was being given a tour of the city.

As the search party was being led into the council chamber, Atar spoke to everyone present. "My, it seems that after four thousand years our island has become a very popular place." All the councilmen smiled at the shared joke. Dismissing the new arrivals' escorts, Atar addressed them. "My name is Atar and these men assembled with me are the council. We are prepared to answer your questions, but first we would like to hear why you have come to our island bearing weapons."

The lieutenant was the first to speak up, "We have come in search of our countrymen whom we believe you have taken hostage."

"Did you feel it necessary to arrive here showing force to gain their freedom? You need not answer that question. I can assure you that our guests have been well taken care of and would have shortly been returned from whence they came had you not intervened. Now we both have a problem," stated Atar.

"What do you mean, we both have a problem?" inquired the befuddled lieutenant.

"We have learned about your warship and the kinds of weapons it carries. If we were to return you to your ship and our guests to their prior location, what assurances have we that your ship or even your country would not wish to retaliate in some destructive way? We only desire to live in peace in our own fashion," Atar continued.

"I can assure you…" started the lieutenant.

"You can assure us nothing, sir. You do not speak as spokesperson of your ship or representative of your nation," Tempest interrupted.

One of the nervous members of the search party blurted out, "If we don't contact our ship soon, it will come here and level this place!"

Tempest stood up, outraged. "Is that some kind of threat?"

Realizing the potential touchy situation they were in, the lieutenant interceded, "No sir, it is not a threat." Tempest then tentatively sat down.

"The boy is a bit nervous. We don't know what you plan to do with us or the others, but he was right about us contacting the ship. If we don't communicate with our ship soon they will set sail for your island. I know you don't want any kind of conflict, but unless we contact our ship soon you may have just that."

Mulling this over for a moment, each councilman linked in thought. Mentally arguing each point, a battlefield of thoughts raced through Atar's mind, with each member giving his advice. Turning his thoughts to the new arrivals, Atar made his decision known. "We will take what you have said under advisement, but for now we ask that you trust us. Relax and enjoy your visit to our city." With a nod, the huge doors to the council chamber opened and four beautiful women stepped in. "These girls will act as your guides and escort. Go and enjoy our simple comforts. Feel free to explore if you wish."

The girls took the bewildered group by their arms and led them out into the city. Activities in the city had increased some since the first group was brought to the island, yet even now the natives gave little notice to the strangers and their strange green garb. The men thought it odd that the citizenry were not as curious as they were about what they were seeing: girls in scantily clad tunics, a palace which abounded in authentic splendor, golden statues, tapestries, and other riches. Now they were brought into a section of the city that resembled the ruins of Egypt, complete with a pyramid—but the pyramid looked almost new and its doorway was open with people coming and going from it.

"Damn strange," the lieutenant murmured while grabbing the shoulder of one of the girls to get her attention. He pointed to the pentagon-shaped building and asked, "What's in there?"

"Would you care to look for yourself and see?" came her reply.

"Yes, we would," answered the lieutenant. With that the girls led them down the cobblestone road to the large three-story structure. Once inside, the group was amazed to see workers busying themselves with the tasks of caring for a variety of animals. Each one or set of animals had its own stall along the outer wall. The stalls looked similar to cells in a prison with a walkway alongside the length of compartments. Looking up the center of the massive building the group saw what was becoming a familiar sight, a blue glowing ceiling. Walking over to the back section of this elaborate habitat, they saw a man working at shifting a tier grouping of grass-like plants and reconnecting hoses of a sort to each tier. As he did so a clear liquid coursed through each hose. The lieutenant nodded. *Hydroponics*, thought the lieutenant.

Noticing the questioning look on the faces of their charges, one of the girls explained, "This is where we breed our animals and maintain a protein source for our community. We have other such buildings devoted to agriculture, atmosphere control, and geothermal energy, if I understand your language properly."

The group was dumbfounded. "Shall we continue our tour of the city?" asked one of the other escorts.

"Y-ye-yes," came the stammering reply from the lieutenant.

The girls then took them down to an area resembling ancient Greece. One of the men thought they were in some kind of time tunnel as they wandered past architecture of different places and periods. That pentagon-shaped building did not resemble any barn any of this group was familiar with. It gave each one an uneasy feeling. *Who are these people?* was the single thought shared by each member of the search party. Eventually they came to an amphitheater where one of the sailors exclaimed, "Hey look!" as he pointed over to a small gathering of men on the opposite side of the amphitheater. "Those must be some of the rig's crew!" he said with excitement. "They're wearing civilian clothes like ours, not this toga and robe crap."

Not caring very much for the way the petty officer was expressing himself, the lieutenant agreed, "You're right, come on, let's get over there." And the group quickened their pace toward the others.

Recognizing their uniforms, the group of men from the oil rig started to walk briskly toward the sailors. As they met, Bob anxiously asked, "Have you come to take us back to our rig?"

"Not exactly, sir," replied the lieutenant with embarrassment. "We were dropped off on this island to reconnoiter and devise a plan to rescue you, but we were captured moments after our copter dropped us off."

"You have a helicopter?" asked Bob.

"Two actually, but a lot of good it's doing us now," remarked the lieutenant in despair. "At any rate, by now our ship should be on its way here."

"Have you seen their weapon?" Paul asked. "Do you honestly think your ship is a match for their energy beam?"

"Yes, I saw the video of your capture and what they are capable of doing, and I do think we are more than a match for them. Our ship was one of the first involved in that Syrian thing. We took out a missile installation, and I'm sure we can take out their weapon system if push comes to shove," the lieutenant boasted.

"Let's hope it doesn't come to that," Steve said sympathetically. "I don't think these people want any kind of confrontation. They explained to us that the reason they took us captive was to learn what to expect from the rest of the surface dwellers."

"Surface dwellers? What kind of talk is that?" asked the lieutenant.

"Oh, then you don't know," remarked Gerald with some astonishment.

"Don't know what?" demanded the lieutenant as his jaw started to tighten. He did not like being kept in the dark about anything.

"You don't know what this place is or where it came from," Gerald answered.

"No, I don't," the lieutenant remarked, his face reddening.

"What I'm about to tell you is going to be hard to believe, but nonetheless, it is true. This is Atlantis, as we call it, and these people have been living at the bottom of the ocean for more than three thousand years," he explained.

"Come oonnnnnn, you expect me to believe that bull?" the lieutenant said mockingly.

Then one of the rig's escorts interrupted them and stated, "What he says is true. Up until a few hours ago we were peacefully living very isolated from you surface dwellers. How else do you explain the presence of an island with a thriving community on it where there was no island before?"

This struck the lieutenant as very odd. It confused him. He could not think of any other possible explanation or any way to answer this young lady.

At this present time the ship had made its way near the island, and at a range of two thousand yards by sonar the captain gave the order to anchor. He had also assembled his officers for another briefing in the wardroom. David was present while they were discussing the best approach from what they saw of the video taken by the helo.

The pilot pointed at the view of the three concentric circles around the island, "This reef is acting like a natural barrier to the island, but there appears to be a way in, see here. There is a gap. Another here on the eastern side of the second ring, and a final one back on the southern side of the inner ring. It appears to be the only navigable way in by boat."

"It could also be a trap," speculated the communications officer. "The thing is a maze, and the prize—the island. You can't tell me they're not expecting us. They've already captured our scouting party."

"What else can we do? We're limited on how many personnel the helo can carry, and another ship couldn't arrive here to assist us before at least another eighteen hours," explained the engineer.

"We could send in a motor whaleboat through the channel with a helo in the air as backup. If anyone from shore should fire at the whaleboat or the copter, the helo should be able to take them out," the executive officer suggested.

Playing the devil's advocate, David asked, "Where would you look or how would you get into the island once you've landed?"

The officers turned toward him and glowered. Then almost ignoring him they turned their attention back to the video.

"That dome must have something to do with it," the captain speculated. "They probably live subterranean. We can see there are no signs of life on the surface of the island. Perhaps if we placed a charge of C-4 near the base we could blow a hole large enough to make an entrance." The officers agreed with the commander's plan. Looking at his watch, he stated, "It is now seventeen hundred hours." Turning to face the engineer, he went on, "I want you to command the assault team. Have your men ready themselves and muster at the motor whaleboat at seventeen-fifteen hours."

"Aye captain, and we'll show them what a destroyer can do," answered the engineer.

To the pilot, the captain said, "Have your men ready the copter with full armaments. I want you to be prepared for anything."

"We'll be ready, sir," the pilot said.

The tension was mounting throughout the ship. Rumors were abounding. This brief fifteen-minute span began to show on the men's already frazzled nerves. When the time finally elapsed, heavily armed men boarded the motor whaleboat. This was the ship's finest assault team. As the craft was launched, the commander gave his final instructions to his men, "Be careful and good luck."

"Thank you, sir," came the engineer's reply. Turning his attention to his men and their tasks, they were off.

Going to the helicopter pad, the captain wished the pilot and his crew good luck as well, and they were off in support of the motor whaleboat. The ships' radar kept constant surveillance of both of the teams. Everything was going well as they drew near the island. The motor whaleboat approached the entrance to the maze of reefs on the island's south side. As it reached the area about sixty feet in front of the entrance, a large blue glowing bubble broached the surface in front of it. Before any of the astonished crew could react, a section of the blue bubble spread open and three men jumped out onto the surface of the bubble. As they did, a small section of the bow melted in front of the startled sailors. No sound, no warning, nothing. One moment it was there, the next moment it was not. Only a melted residue gave any indication that something was there previously.

"Look there!" shouted the surprised copilot pointing to a large blue bubble-shaped thing in front of the motor whaleboat. Before the pilot could react, he saw three men pop out of the strange craft. As the copter came in for a closer look, the pilot noticed that a portion of the bow was missing.

One of the assault team regained control of his senses and grabbed his radio, "Rainbow-One we've been fired upon."

The pilot didn't know what to do. The alien craft was too close to the whaleboat to fire upon without taking the risk of possibly hitting the boat as well.

The USS Lavan was monitoring the communications between the assault team and the helo. Upon hearing "we've been fired upon," the captain gave the order to sound general quarters. Over the 1-MC came a loud continuous bonging sound for about five seconds followed by, "General Quarters, General Quarters, all hands man your battle stations. This is not a drill!"

When the men aboard the ship heard the words "This is not a drill," it was as if they all kicked in their afterburners and in less than a minute the bridge received reports that all stations were manned and ready.

"Get the anchor up!" yelled the captain.

The familiar police whistle blew, followed by, "Underway—shift colors," and the USS Lavan was on its way to aid their comrades under fire.

"Prepare to launch a stinger missile at hostile craft," ordered the pilot to the copilot who then armed the fire control system.

"I don't think we can get a clear shot. The alien craft is too close. We might hit our own vessel," replied the copilot as he sighted in the alien bubble.

"Rainbow-One to Lavan, hostile craft is too close to attempt firing—awaiting your instructions," requested the pilot.

"Lavan aye, wait-one," came the reply. Before the captain could give any kind of instruction, the pilot called back.

"Rainbow-One to Lavan. They're gone!"

"Repeat your last, Rainbow-One," requested the communications officer.

"They're gone!" replied the pilot, half stunned. "Before we could react, our men boarded the alien craft and now they're gone—submerged—vanished!" the pilot stated.

"Return to the ship!" ordered the captain angrily. Turning to face the communications officer, the captain quickly ordered him to send a message.

CHAPTER TEN

Across the ocean on a fax machine at the communication center in Norfolk, Virginia the following message was received:

CLASS: Top Secret - Eyes Only
FLASH-OP IMMEDIATE
1824 14 June 2021
From: Commanding Officer, USS Lavan
To: President, USA
             SecDef
             CNO
             ComLantFlt
Info: AIG 159.1
Subj: Verified New Island.
             Inhabited, Hostile.
             Search Party, fired upon.
             Require Assistance.
             Awaiting further orders.

An alarm went off indicating the urgency of the message. The radioman on duty picked up the message and began to read. Without hesitation she took the message, logged in the time it arrived, and then quickly went to the phone. First, she called the Commander of the Atlantic Fleet, followed by the office of the Chief of Naval Operations, then the Secretary of Defense, and finally the President of the United States. This was the order used to ensure each department head was kept informed before his superior was notified and the department head held responsible for the proper response to the events mentioned in the message. Upon receipt of the transmittal, the president called an emergency meeting of the National Security Council. Within an hour they were all assembled in the blue room.

"I'm sure you have heard of the encounter the *USS Lavan* had earlier today. What do you propose we do about it?" the president asked.

"The sixth fleet in the Mediterranean can be ordered to their location for assistance," suggested the CNO. "The Mideast situation is pretty much self-contained at present."

"Then what, level the island and kill a number of Americans? I don't think so." Leaning on the table with his palms spread out and head bowed, the president thought for a moment before saying, "Perhaps we could handle this situation like Reagan did Grenada. Send in six thousand marines and storm the island."

"Or we could do what President Obama did and send in Seal Team Six," suggested the Secretary of Defense. "I'm sure they could extract the hostages safely."

"Only if they knew the layout of the land," remarked the CNO.

"Why can't we provide them with that information? We have enough satellites in the area," commented the Commander of the Atlantic Fleet.

The next few hours went by with the men discussing different tactical situations and scenarios. Then came a knock on the door and the president's secretary entered and gave him another Flash-Op Immediate message.

The newest captives were brought before the council and immediately Dawson, the boisterous engineer, demanded, "What have you done with the others?"

Calmly Atar stood up and addressed them, "Welcome, I am Atar, leader of the council and I can assure you that all our guests are being well cared for."

"Guests!" Dawson fumed, "What guests? You've taken us prisoner."

"We have detained you, yes, but you are not prisoners," assured Atar.

"If we're not prisoners then we can go, correct?" he asked.

"Yes and no," replied Atar. "You may go back to your ship, but your men will remain here as our guests until we can resolve this situation we are in with your country."

"So we are prisoners," quarreled the engineer.

"If you wish to think of it that way. Your men will have free access to our city. They may go and visit any part as they choose. An escort will be provided so that they will not get lost. Quite frankly, our city is a maze. We will prepare a meal for them and perhaps by that time you will return from your mission."

"My mission! What mission?" the dumbfounded engineer inquired.

"You will be taken back to your ship. You may then apprise them of your situation and that of your men. One of our scouts will accompany you to explain our part in this predicament along with one of the rig's crewmen. He will go to attest to our hospitality and fair treatment. Your task is twofold; one, and most importantly, to assure the safety of our scout, and two, to invite your captain to come before our council so that we may attempt to settle this misunderstanding. We further request that a representative of your government be sent to help arrange an official settlement with your government. We fervently wish for no hostile actions by either party."

"No hostile actions! What do you call shooting off our bow and capturing innocent civilians?"

"You are unaware of all the facts to judge our actions, and our 'shooting off your bow,' as you say, was a necessary response to prevent your people from firing at us and starting a needless battle. We do not wish to hurt anyone, and so far we have accomplished this."

Dawson, now defensive, demanded, "Is that some kind of a threat?"

"No, *a fact*," Atar bluntly stated.

"Raval, take the man named Bob Robinson from the rig and this officer to his ship. Explain to his commander what is needed and return with him as soon as is convenient." He nodded toward Raval who returned the gesture.

"Come, we must go," instructed Raval to the engineer. "You need not worry about your men. No harm shall befall them."

"Where's this Bob Robinson we're supposed to take with us?" inquired the officer.

"He is awaiting us now near my scoutcraft," answered Raval, showing no sign of emotion.

The two made their way through the streets to the waterfront area. This small cove was the Atlantian's only link with the outside world. It once was a vent to the ancient volcano, but became sealed three millennia earlier. When they arrived at the scoutcraft, Bob Robinson stood up from the steps he had been sitting on near the Atlantian vessel. He had been instructed to wait there until Raval arrived. Raval's crew had already made all the necessary preparations for getting underway; when the three of them came aboard they departed.

Upon clearing the maze of reef, the craft made its silent way to where the engineer's ship was located. Matching its course and speed, Raval's crew surfaced the scoutcraft just a few feet from the ship's port side without being detected. Raval strode to one end of the blue bubble craft and an opening appeared. Dawson was the first to climb onto the surface of this strange spherical craft, closely followed by Raval and Bob. Hearing the engineer's hail, the portside lookout immediately called for the captain. After a few quick verbal exchanges, the commander had a ladder lowered so the three could come aboard. Once they were safely aboard, the scoutcraft submerged and all traces of it disappeared. Sonar couldn't pick it up even when they went active.

"Where did your vessel go?" Bob asked Raval.

"Not far, I assure you," came his reply with a half-smile. "It will return when I am ready to depart."

Taking the group to his stateroom, the captain inquired, "Who are they?"

Before the engineer could speak, the Atlantian answered, "I am Raval. I have been sent to invite you to come before our council. Their wish is to resolve this misunderstanding before anyone comes to harm."

"Misunderstanding?" Commander Wells snapped with sarcasm. "Your people have kidnapped innocent civilians, and captured and fired upon members of the U.S. Navy. I would say this is more than a misunderstanding."

"However you interpret it, I have been sent to persuade you to meet with the leaders of the island. I am prepared to give you an explanation of the past two revolutions of this planet," Raval offered.

"Does he always talk that way—'revolutions of this planet'?" Dawson whispered to Bob.

"You don't know the half of it," Bob replied.

"You may continue," the captain stated in a dismissive tone.

"As you wish," Raval replied with a calm, even voice. "My island was once resting at the bottom of this body of water. Our soothsayers predicted a massive earthquake that would soon destroy our home...."

For the next thirty minutes he went on with his tale about the events that led to the tidal wave, the abduction of the rig's crew, and the subsequent capture of the search party and rescue team. He concluded with an invitation for the captain to meet with the council, and a request that a representative of their government meet with them as well. Raval now waited expectantly.

The commander, now a bit more knowledgeable about the Atlantian's situation, became more receptive and less sarcastic. Calling for the communications officer to join them, he asked Bob, "Have they harmed any of your men?"

"No, except for being taken at gun point, they have treated us most graciously. They have even allowed us to explore their city," came Bob's reply.

Turning to Dawson, he asked, "How about your men? Any injuries?"

"No sir. No one injured. Some shock, though."

The communications officer knocked, then entered the CO's stateroom, "Yes sir, you called for me?"

"Yes, I need another flash message sent. Address it the same as the last one. State that island's leaders wish to talk with a U.S. representative about terms for releasing all hostages. They require assurance of non-retaliation before the hostages will be released. Inform them we are awaiting confirmation of this request and their ETA to this location. Send the message now and await their reply. I'll be in my stateroom until then."

The coms officer eagerly wrote down the message. "Aye sir, I'll send this out straight away."

Looking at his watch, the commander offered Raval a drink. This he accepted as a curiosity, wondering how this beverage compared with that of his home's familiar nectar. After taking a sip he casually remarked, "Palatable," before downing the rest.

Bob began to salivate. He sure could use a drink too. The captain, pleased with Raval's response, offered both the engineer and Bob a glass as he poured one for himself.

The president accepted the second message from his secretary and read it immediately. His council remained silent as he did so.

"Gentlemen, we have a break in that hostage situation. The leaders on that island are willing to negotiate a peaceful release of all hostages with one of our representatives." Turning to face Secretary of State Arthur Franks, the president continued, "Arthur, I want you to go down there and mediate their release. *Air Force One* will fly you down to Norfolk, NAS, and from there one of our long range helicopters will take you to the *Lavan* which is anchored off the coast of that island."

The CNO interrupted, "Find out what you can about their military strength, just in case."

"That will be enough!" retorted the president. "These people, whoever they may be, have opened their hand to us for a peaceful settlement. I will not jeopardize a chance for peaceful relations just to satisfy a curiosity of power." The president called in his private secretary and instructed, "Send a message back to the *USS Lavan* that the Secretary of State will arrive sometime tomorrow afternoon their time."

Raval had enjoyed the drink and followed the captain to the wardroom where he was able to partake of some of the delicacies the ship's pantries could offer. It was the dinner hour and most of the ship's officers were now eating, with Raval seated at the captain's right-hand side. Much of the conversation was routine with a few questions about the island directed to Raval. Everyone noticed the odd-looking garb he was wearing, and that he did not appear to be too unlike them in appearance; maybe a little taller and leaner, but not too different. It also made the men more at ease that Raval could speak English very clearly, and surprised some of them how well he understood technical information and Navy jargon. Little did they know that Raval was one of the elite chosen who could read minds. His quick wit and adaptability was one reason the council chose him to represent their people.

The only thing really unsettling was his seeming lack of humor and solemn attitude. It was almost surprising how well the officers were treating him in view of the fact that his people had captured some of their shipmates, but the captain maintained a friendly atmosphere, having had his share of fostering diplomatic relations during his career.

After dinner the commander offered Raval a cigar, which he chose to decline. Oblivious to Raval's reasoning, the captain lit his cigar, permitting the other officers to light their various smoking materials. "If you will excuse me, captain, I wish to go on deck for some fresh air. I am unused to this pollution your kind seems to revel in," Raval remarked with unprecedented disdain.

Becoming self-conscious, the commander's face turned red. "Yes, of course. Dawson, please escort our guest on deck," requested the captain of his engineer.

There remained no sign of the strange blue bubble craft as dusk arrived. In the distance an amethyst sky blossomed across the horizon.

One of the radiomen came to the wardroom bringing the captain the latest message traffic. It included the president's communiqué to him about the Secretary of State's arrival the next day. He, in turn, informed the executive officer and the others in the wardroom, instructing them to have the crew field day the ship first thing after morning muster in preparation for the secretary's arrival. Extinguishing his cigar, he went in search of Dawson and Raval.

Finding them on the port side 01 level, the captain informed them, "I've just received word that the Secretary of State is on his way here and should arrive sometime tomorrow afternoon." Facing Raval he continued, "The Secretary of State is our government's representative and he is coming at your request to talk with your leaders about our crewmen and those civilian workers' release."

"That is well," replied Raval. "Would you care to arrange for your crewmen's release at this hour?"

Stunned by the Atlantian's question, the captain was taken aback for a moment. Collecting himself he replied, "Yes, I would, but how?"

"Do not panic at what you are about to see. Just follow me and we shall go to the island," instructed Raval as he walked to the rail.

How? questioned the captain. "I must tell my crew that I am going."

Raval said curtly, "Your engineer can inform your crew." Then lowering his head ever so slightly toward the water, he closed his eyes for a brief moment. When his eyes opened the silent blue bubble surfaced next to the ship's gangway. "Follow me," was all Raval said.

Though surprised, the captain stepped down to the noiseless submersible. *How could this be possible? How?* he contemplated.

The engineer's mouth fell open. The suddenness of the blue bubble's arrival placed him in a temporary state of shock. All he could do was watch his commander climb aboard. Even the lookout didn't notice what was happening. The event occurred too suddenly and quietly for anyone to notice—anyone except Bob. When he saw his ride about to depart he shouted, "Wait for me!" then sprang down the ladder and into the submersible. In a moment they were gone. Raval, Bob, the captain, and the blue bubble vanished.

Regaining his senses only after the strange craft disappeared; the engineer immediately went to the bridge to report the captain's absence.

The ship's landing party had been escorted into the city shortly after the engineer departed with Raval. Once inside, they were allowed to roam free and wander about without any escort. After discovering the surface dweller's limitations, the council determined that they were incapable of harming or interfering with their work or the island's citizens, and so they were afforded total freedom in the city. It was amazing how quickly some of the sailors found their way to a local pub. It was, in fact, a gathering place for the island's inhabitants to meet, drink, and socialize after they had completed their daily tasks. There the seamen were offered the same strong drink those from the oil rig had an opportunity to sample earlier. Though eager to accept this unusual nectar, they sipped at their goblets experimentally at first. Once they were assured that these drinks were palatable, they commenced to consume their fill. The Atlantians thought it amusing to see these strangers fall under the influence of their brew. A chief petty officer tried to down his goblet in one swallow, and almost made it, only to spit out the last few drops when he burst into laughter, amused by his absurd feat. In a short time these three were hardly in any shape to walk.

One of Hellena's girlfriends happened to pass by about the same moment the sailors decided to move on. She was also amused by their staggering behavior, but felt strangely attracted to one of them. He was tall, blonde, and in her opinion, very handsome. Much more so, she thought, than the one named Steve.

Brashly walking up to him, she introduced herself. "My name is Sara. What is your name?"

"John Michael," he replied as he stood there smiling and leaning a bit to his right. Remembering his manners, he quickly added, "Ma'am."

Sara smiled, musing, *It's amusing that he endeavored to remember his manners when addressing a lady. Especially in the state he is in.*

"Would you like me to show you around our city?" she asked.

"Yes—please," came his slurred reply.

Taking him by his hand she led him away from the pub. His two buddies were overwhelmed that such a gorgeous woman would just introduce herself and leave with one of them. "Now that's what I call friendly!" exclaimed Joe Bob, one of John's friends.

The other added, "Now that's what I call woman—whooweee!"

Sara took John deep into the city, showing him the various architectural designs used throughout. Her conversation centered on the island's past, while he discussed what he could remember about world history. Making their way around the back streets toward the citadel, Sara took John up to her residence. He was very impressed with its furnishings and surprised to see how similar it looked to most apartments back home. The oddest thing was the walls. They seemed to be aglow, illuminating the entire room. No other light source was visible. No lamp of any kind. "Make yourself comfortable," Sara instructed.

Spotting a couch, he walked over and sat and found it to be very soft and comfortable. As he sat his eyelids became heavy. He hadn't realized how tired he was. Before he entered the land of nod, Sara came over and placed her hand on his. "Tired?" she mewed. John nodded affirmatively.

"It must be the drink. We have found that outsiders are unable to cope well with its effects." John just grinned. He liked the euphoric feeling he felt from that strange brew. He was still feeling a buzz and very uninhibited when he pulled Sara over to him and gave her a very wet, passionate kiss. Her response was instant, putting her arms around him to tighten their embrace.

When they finally broke their caress, John pulled his head back so he could focus his eyes better on her lanky, soft-looking body. She simply gazed deep into his blue eyes. He was impressed by her very skimpy tunic, and by how it actually covered very little of her body. He was feeling a bit warm now, almost overheated. Removing his shirt, he embraced her in his arms once more to kiss her rosy, soft lips. While in the embrace he began roaming the contours of her body with his hands. As his hands slipped beneath her tunic they came to a familiar spot, cupping one of her firm breasts. Passions rose as their kissing became frantic; all the while they continued their heavy petting. Sliding his hand around her back, his hand came to her side and felt something strange yet oddly familiar in some way. His fingers came to a warm moist spot. *Nah, it can't be*, he presumed. *Not a pussy!*

As he slid his fingers into the moist, soft, fleshy part of her side, she coughed. Startled, John jumped back breaking their embrace, his eyes widening with bewilderment.

"Wha-wha-whaaat'ssss that?" he stammered.

Calmly she explained, "My gills."

Gills? John puzzled, and then suddenly stuttered, "G-g-g-gillls?"

"Yes, John," she remarked quite frankly, "I can breathe underwater as well as in the air."

"Wow!" then he thought, *That's neat!*

Undaunted and still in bit of a stupor, John leaned over and drew her to him, continuing his passionate embrace and heavy petting. They were both getting very excited. At that moment neither could settle for just fondling each other, so Sara stood up in front of John's gaping gaze and pulled her tunic off, revealing two of the most beautiful breasts he had ever seen. Her body was perfectly proportioned. In no time at all he stripped down to match her nakedness and climbed into her waiting arms. After thrashing about on the couch for a while, Sara announced, "This just won't do," and took John by the hand, quickly leading him into her bed.

Without hesitation they continued their lovemaking, uninterrupted until they both climaxed in a spasm of pleasure. John, exhausted from all his activity and still feeling the sedative effects of that strange brew, rolled off her and soon fell asleep.

The captain was escorted before the assembled council and heard what had become a familiar greeting, "Welcome, I am Atar, leader of the council. We are glad you have come."

"I understand that we can negotiate the release of my men. Is that true?"

"That is correct, captain," replied Atar. "Has Raval explained to you our present situation and the reasoning behind our actions?"

"Yes, he has, and as I understand it you have your answers, so why not release everyone, if that was your original intent?" remarked Captain Wells.

"We fear that by not understanding our situation your country may decide to retaliate. We have no desire to commence hostilities. On the contrary, we wish to establish peaceful trade and exchanges of culture," Atar explained. "We do not wish to release everyone until we have obtained some kind of assurance from your government."

"What about my men?"

"If you wish, I can have your men assembled here in the morning. You see we have given them unrestricted access to our city, and it will take a bit of time to locate their whereabouts and direct them back here," Atar explained.

"Yes, I would like that," replied Commander Wells in a more relaxed manner, "but what about me?"

Atar turned his attention to Raval and the two guards at the door, and with a nod they departed the hall. "Raval will assemble your men, and I can assure you of their well-being," Atar claimed politely.

Hellena came into the chamber shortly after Raval had departed. Gesturing her to step closer, Atar went on to say, "In the meantime, my daughter will give you a tour of our city. We should have your men gathered by your return."

"Thank you," came the captain's gracious reply.

An hour after their passionate lovemaking, Sara placed her hand on John's shoulder and woke him with a shake. "It is time for you to go."

Groggy, he awoke, stretched, yawned, and asked the first thought that came to his bewildered mind. "Why?" he whined.

"Your captain is on his way to this island to retrieve his men. You can wait with the others at our meeting place," she told him.

"What if I don't want to go?" he asked.

Pushing him out of bed, she asserted, "You must." John landed on the floor with a thud.

Gathering his clothes, though still in a semi-groggy state, he dressed, all the while protesting her forcing him to leave. A smile then came to his lips as he remembered the previous hours of lovemaking. How many people could say they'd made love to a mermaid?

Once dressed, Sara escorted him down toward the Atlantian's meeting area. Seeing some of his friends still where he had left them a couple of hours ago, he sauntered over to them on his own. Sara departed, grinning at her paramour.

As he stepped to their table, his friends offered him another drink.

Without a second thought he gladly accepted. After a few swallows, and his friends nagging him to tell them what he'd been up to the past two hours, he told them in graphic detail.

"Oh, come on!" exclaimed Joe Bob. "You expect us to believe *that?*"

Within the hour Raval had personally located each member of the ship's complement, including John Michael, who was still feeling the effects of that unusual green brew. Atar's daughter concluded her gracious tour of the citadel with the captain and directed him back to the council chambers. When they entered the room the captain was pleased to find his men present. More than half of them were drunk, having imbibed the Atlantian's drink.

"I regret the condition that some of your men are in, captain. They apparently have taken full advantage of our hospitality. It appears your kind cannot handle our drink very well. It is a strong brew indeed," remarked Atar.

"You can say that again!" Joe Bob hollered. The captain was somewhat embarrassed by the way his men were conducting themselves. It did not look well for the Navy.

"Raval and his crew are ready to return you and your men to your vessel. Raval has been instructed to wait there until the arrival of your country's representative and then to escort him before the council. At that time we shall discuss the return of the others. As you can see, we have harmed no one and have treated them well and with open arms," explained Atar.

"I'll say!" shouted Ed, another of the drunken sailors, in agreement.

The captain was getting a bit angry with the conduct of his crew and shouted, "Attention!" Some almost fell over in an attempt to comply with his order. Thoroughly steamed by now, the captain redressed them, "You are lucky I don't bring the lot of you up on charges of dereliction of duty!" This got the men's attention. "Follow me to the submersible. You're going back to the ship. At ease!" With a sigh of relief, the men relaxed. "Follow me!" the captain barked, then guided his men down to the waterfront and the awaiting Atlantian transport.

CHAPTER ELEVEN

The following afternoon Secretary of State Arthur Franks flew by helicopter to the *USS Lavan*. The minute he was aboard, the captain greeted and directed him to the wardroom to meet with his officers. Seating himself to relax from his hectic flight, he was all business and asked, "What is the present situation?"

Without pause or in any way trying to describe the events of the past few days, the captain bluntly replied, "My men have been returned to the ship, yet the Atlantians still hold the rig's crew hostage, sir."

"Atlantians?" interrupted the befuddled Secretary of State. "Are you saying these people on this island claim to be from Atlantis?"

"Yes sir," the commander answered. "From all that I have seen and heard that *is* Atlantis."

"What makes you think such a ridiculous thought? Atlantians indeed! Are you insane?"

"No sir, I am not. If I may, I can show you a video taken on the oil rig that recorded the events leading to the abduction of its crew." Finding the controls of the video system, Commander Wells pushed in the DVD and pressed play. The TV mounted on the bulkhead illuminated, displaying the events of the other night. When the video ended the captain added, "There was a small tidal wave that hit the rig a couple of hours before these events. Much of the crew was involved in effecting repairs when the alien submersible arrived. You have seen what their weapon can do and I have been on their craft. It's like nothing else on earth. There were no visible controls, yet they maneuvered this thing alongside my ship on a parallel course and matched the ship's speed precisely. I was taken to their island last night myself where I arranged for my crew's return."

"You went over there?" Arthur remarked with surprise.

"Yes, I was told by one of them that his leaders would discuss the return of my men and I was persuaded to go. I have seen their city. It's magnificent! Like something almost timeless. When I talked with them I found out how they came to the surface. I am confident that they are Atlantians and that they are sincere in their wish for peaceful relations. Sir, if I can be frank with you, I feel we have a unique opportunity here to exchange cultural ideologies and technologies."

"Are you such an authority on Atlantis? What makes you think this isn't some kind of elaborate hoax to make the U.S. look foolish?" inquired the diplomat.

"But sir, there was never an island on any charts at this location, yet now there is one here. How do you explain that?" Commander Wells challenged.

The secretary was astounded, and couldn't think of an answer, so he asked, "Why did they capture the crew of that oil rig, and why, if they are so damn friendly, haven't they released them yet?" Arthur was getting upset. Irritable and tired from his long flight, coupled with all this nonsense about Atlantis, he found all this a bit much.

Commander Wells looked him straight in the eye and explained why the Atlantians did what they did as it had been explained to him. It surprised the captain how well he remembered the Atlantian's words as he performed this recitation. Then to answer the secretary he concluded, "They are waiting for confirmation that no retaliatory acts will befall them for their actions. They further wish to establish trade and economic relations as well as exchange of scientific information." Addressing the engineer, the captain ordered, "Send Raval in."

Bewildered, the Secretary of State asked, "Who is Raval?"

"Raval is the island's representative," replied the commander. In moments a tall slender man with dark hair wearing a long, black nightshirt-looking outfit entered the wardroom with the engineer bringing up the rear. Walking straight to the secretary, the Atlantian introduced himself and offered his hand in friendship. "I am Raval and you must be the one I have waited for to escort to the elders."

"Ye-ye-yes, I am," stammered the secretary in bewilderment that Raval should know who he was. "How did you know I am the one?"

Answering, Raval replied in a flat expression, "Your dress is different than the others, and I was introduced to the others in this room earlier." Allowing a moment for that thought to sink in, Raval then said, "If you are prepared, I can take you to the island to meet with the Council of Elders."

Turning to look at the commander, the secretary asked in a whisper, "Do you think it's safe?"

The captain replied in a low voice, "Yes."

"Very well, errr Mr. Raval, is it? I shall go with you now."

"Please follow me." Raval led the secretary, captain, and the rest of the curious wardroom to the port side of the ship near the accommodation ladder. Standing by the railing, Raval nodded his head toward the water. In response to his summons, the now-familiar large blue submersible broached the surface and was alongside the naval vessel. Returning his attention to the Secretary of State, Raval announced, "If you will follow me I will take you to my island."

Arthur was beside himself. Seeing a blue bubble on a monitor was one thing. Seeing it in person was quite another, yet he managed to control himself and not ask foolish questions. As Raval approached the craft a portion of its surface slid away, and without breaking his stride, he climbed onboard the craft with the now very nervous Secretary of State behind him.

"I'm coming along," stated the captain firmly as he bounded down the ladder on the heels of the secretary. Once aboard, the open section of the bubble sealed itself and they were on their way.

The trip to the island was amazingly brief; and, once there, Mr.

Franks was escorted directly to the council chamber. As they entered the great hall from a doorway far to the rear, the councilmen began to assemble. Once each was in his place and seated, Atar spoke his greeting, "Welcome, I am Atar, leader of the Council of Elders. We have anxiously awaited your arrival. Please take a seat." Atar gestured to the chairs situated in front of their table. "Refresh yourself for we have much we wish to discuss with you." At his signal a servant brought in a tray filled with assorted delicacies and some drink.

Commander Wells leaned over and whispered into the secretary's ear, "Be careful with that stuff. I have three men onboard comatose, and one man a bit deranged. He swears he saw a mermaid."

Arthur grinned and nodded as he grabbed a piece of strange-looking fruit. "This tastes great. It's very unusual. What do you call it?" he inquired, looking up at Atar.

Atar answered, "Sukara. Have you not such a food as this?"

The secretary's straightforward reply was, "No, in fact there is a lot here that is hard to understand," as he listed all the unsettling things he had noticed during his excursion. "First, this place, your island, it hadn't existed until about two days ago, and if what I have been told is true, you have risen from the ocean's bottom. How is it that you speak our language?"

Before Atar or any of the council could answer, he blurted out, "And why have you captured the men off our oil rig, and now hold them hostage...?" Arthur's face became firm as stone as he fixed his eyes on Atar.

Tempest could restrain himself no longer, and broke into the secretary's tirade. "What gives you the right to accuse us of such a barbaric act? These men are our guests, and have been treated as such," Tempest sternly expounded. "No harm has come to them. In fact, we have given them free rein over the city. It is your hostile act of impending retaliation that drove us to send for a representative of your government."

"These men may go as soon as we have finished our summit meeting," Mord added.

Atar raised his hand in gesture. Both Tempest and Mord sat back in their seats as Atar returned his attention to their distinguished guest and replied in a calm voice, "Please excuse my fellow countrymen. The mere fact that we must meet with you is unsettling. To answer your question, our city has indeed risen from the depths of this great body of water. We speak many languages quite well, and we speak English now because it is your tongue. We believe our own language is the original speech spoken upon this world, and all other languages are forms or dialects of our own. We learned these in times past when one of our workers discovered sounds being produced from crystals being cut by a low power maser. Somehow we picked up transmissions from above. From these we familiarized ourselves with many forms of communication."

Atar continued his explanation, "We have lived contentedly for many millennia at the bottom of this vast expanse of water. We survived. By the grace of the gods a catastrophe had turned into a victory. By necessity, our isolation accelerated our development of certain of the sciences. We not only survived, we prospered. Then quite recently an accident activated our once-extinct volcano and hurtled us to the surface. We needed answers to many questions in the shortest amount of time possible. It was that need that prompted us to send our scout ships to retrieve the first beings they encountered so we could obtain information as to what kind of world we had been hurled into. What kind of men are they? Who now rules? What is our best course of action?"

Atar paused to take a drink from his goblet, his eyes leaving the secretary's only for a brief moment. The room was still and quiet. All the members of the council were staring at the diplomat. Once Atar's thirst was satiated, he continued, "That is why these men were brought here. As to why they have not yet been returned, your warship arrived before we could find out what we needed to know. They remain here as our guests until we can make certain that there will be no retaliation by your government. We wish to establish commerce and trade of goods and ideas between our people and that of the surface dwellers." Atar caught his last statement. Not wishing to offend this representative, he apologetically said, "I am sorry. Perhaps we should no longer use the term *surface dweller* as it appears that we too now dwell once more with the sky."

Arthur noticed his chance to be diplomatic and replied, "No offense taken, sir."

Atar accepted his statement with a grin and continued, "So now perhaps you can better understand our position and why we took the actions we did when we did. I am sure if the roles had been reversed you would have acted similarly."

"I can see your reasoning, but may I be allowed to speak with the men from the rig?" asked the secretary.

"We have anticipated your request, and have sent for the nominal leader of their group. I am informed that he has been contacted and is on his way here now. Is there anything else we can do for you at this time?"

Arthur sat back in his chair and thought for a moment, but before he could answer, the great doors to the council chamber swung open and Bob entered the room with his escort, Sue. Spotting the familiar naval uniform, Bob headed straight toward the captain. Both he and the secretary stood up to greet him, as Bob put out his hand to the two, saying, "Does this mean you have come for me and my men?"

Before either could answer, Tempest interjected, "In due course. We first require some assurances from your Secretary of State."

Arthur turned his head toward Tempest and just glared at him, then turned to Bob and asked, "How are you and your men?"

"Not too bad considering I was yanked from the best party I've been to this century. They've treated us like royalty since we got here, but I don't think they found out everything they wanted to know from us," he replied.

Glancing at Commander Wells then back to Bob, Arthur stated with pride, "Now that we are here everything is under control. You and your men will soon be on your way back to your rig." Turning to face Atar, the secretary exclaimed, "If all the men tell me the same, that they have been treated well, I can give you the assurances that you want. There will be no retaliation, and I will explain to my government why you took the course of action you did."

"Very well," replied Atar. "Now if you will please follow me I shall personally escort you around our city and show you some of the benefits we shall share with your people. We offer what we have free to all people." As Atar stood so did the rest of the assembly. "I shall have the other men from the rig gather here by our return." Atar nodded toward Mord, who bowed in return before departing the council chamber. Atar then led the secretary and captain out the tall side doors of the great hall that led to the center of the city.

"I'll wait here for my men, if it's alright with you," requested Bob.

Atar nodded and said, "That is good. Sue shall keep you company." At that the trio departed out the door. Atar guided them through the maze of buildings that made up the city. He pointed out the various types of architecture and explained, "We have learned much in the ways of constructing buildings." A short while later Atar led them to a pyramid-shaped structure across from what looked like a statue of a large, beautiful mermaid. Once inside he began to describe some of Atlantis' history before the great holocaust.

"Our people sailed around the world. We were very much at home in the sea even then. In our travels my forefathers discovered this island and here established a base of operation. In this place they experimented and dreamt the dream of a world tamed by mankind. A world where man could adapt or evolve into a being that would thrive in any hostile environment nature could produce. We discovered many kinds of medicines and cures for most ills. Our most recent discovery lay at the base of our island. There is a plant that grows down there, yet not just a plant, it is also part animal. We have learned to cultivate it and extract a substance that not only enhances the immune system, but also increases longevity." Looking directly at the secretary, he paused to ask, "Am I boring you?"

"No, not really. I find it quite interesting," he replied.

"How old do you think I am?" Atar inquired.

The secretary considered for a moment while scrutinizing Atar's face and hands before commenting, "Around eighty. Maybe as old as eighty seven," trying to hedge his bet and claim a few more years than his appearance reflected.

"Why thank you," Atar replied. "I am 238 years old, as you record time."

Both of the outworlder's mouths fell open in disbelief. They remained silent for a while, shocked by this declaration. It was too much for either of them to comprehend or accept. Atar barely looked eighty. His posture was perfect, and his stride took effort on both their parts to keep up with him. Finally, Commander Wells found his voice and asked, "Are you serious? You are really 238 years old?"

"That is correct. You must believe everything that I tell you," Atar stated with bluntness.

Arthur returned to his senses and inquired, "Will this substance work on people like me?

"Yes, but it works best if introduced in the fetal stage of development."

The secretary's mind reeled with the possibilities this substance could provide. *Perhaps it could be synthesized. Maybe it could cure AIDS.* Then he asked, "Could this substance cure AIDS?"

"What is aids?" asked Atar.

The secretary raised his brow, thinking, *Wouldn't it be wonderful if the next generation could ask that too—what is AIDS?* In an attempt to explain, he stated, "AIDS is an acronym we use for Acquired Immune Deficiency Syndrome. It is a disease that attacks the immune system and makes it virtually useless. The next disease you catch can kill you."

"I understand. I believe this substance could help, but you would have to discuss this with one of our life science students." Thinking for a moment, Atar suggested, "Oman would know for sure, but until I send for him perhaps one of his students could help you. That is why I have brought you to this place—to discuss with our people what your people's needs are, so that we could prepare an exchange of knowledge. This is our life science building. Everything pertaining to life is studied and developed here."

As he spoke a beautiful, young looking brunette woman approached the trio, and bowed respectfully to Atar. Then she introduced herself to the others. "I am Nena. I understand that you have questions about some of our developments here."

"Yes, I do," replied the secretary with enthusiasm. "Around the world there is an epidemic of a disease we call AIDS as well as other immuno-deficiency diseases. In the case of AIDS, it is a disease which attacks the immune system rendering it useless. Then any illness one acquires afterwards is nearly always fatal. Atar was telling us of a compound that enhances the immune system as well as promoting longevity. Do you think that this substance could cure those afflicted with this disease?"

"If I correctly understand you, I believe it could. If not, we have the ability to alter this substance's structure so that it would, in fact, destroy the disease and then effectively be used to inoculate the remainder of the world. We could eliminate that disease entirely, but we will require fresh blood samples from both a healthy surface dweller and one infected with the disease. Can you arrange this?"

The secretary was flabbergasted. Here he was on a mission to arrange the release of American hostages, and their captors have the cure to the world's most dreaded disease. *If I can arrange to attain this new wonder serum I'll be a national hero.* Returning from his reverie he answered her. "I can arrange this. If you want I can obtain volunteers to donate blood from the very healthy men onboard our ship, so you could get started right away. I can obtain an AIDS victim within a few days."

"Could you arrange for a volunteer to remain here for a period of time?" Nena requested. "It would allow us an opportunity to do some comparative studies, and thus be able to help you better."

"Yes, that can be arranged," said the secretary bluntly, thinking all the time how well this would look on his report in Washington.

Atar interjected into the conversation, "I have received word that your men have been assembled and await us in the council chambers. We should return now." Neither man noticed anyone come to Atar with any kind of message, which made them curiously puzzled. He had been standing quietly off to the side ever since Nena introduced herself.

"Alright," Arthur answered with visions of returning to the president with a negotiated deal for the cure to AIDS dancing through his head.

The trio made their way back along the maze of buildings; only it seemed to be a different route. Atar pointed to other interestingly shaped structures and explained how each shape represented a different field of study or industry. Later they found out that the housing was located in the outer parameter of the city.

This time they approached the citadel from what the two outsiders thought to be the rear. They walked through a passageway which took them past many closed doors. Atar explained, "These are suites. Some are guest rooms, though before this day we have had little use for them."

Bob greeted them upon their arrival to the council chamber, and introduced the other captives. The secretary did his diplomatic best to shake every man's hand. "How are you doing?" he asked each one.

Most of the men said pretty much the same thing that Bob reported earlier. Paul was the only exception. He complained about everything, and demanded to know when they were going to be released. The secretary took this in stride and explained the details of their release to him and the process that would return them to their rig. While in the middle of his explanation, the large doors at the entrance to the chamber swung open. Raval and a petty officer from the ship entered the room.

The sailor stepped briskly up to the captain, saluted, and recited his memorized message. "The Officer of the Deck sends his respects and wishes to report ECM contact with a Russian cruiser heading toward this island."

"Why wasn't this report sent by hand radio?" the commander demanded.

"The ship has been trying to get in contact with you for the past half hour, sir. When they couldn't get through to you, the OOD decided to send me."

"I understand. Thank you. Return to the ship and have him prepare to get underway and to receive the landing party and the others," instructed the commander.

"Have the OOD prepare to get underway, and prepare to receive the landing part and the others, aye sir," the sailor acknowledged while saluting the captain. After his salute was returned, the sailor did an about face and departed the citadel.

Atar, in all innocence, spoke up and asked, "What are these Russians and ECM?"

The captain looked at the secretary then back to Atar before answering, "The Russians are a people whose nation we oppose politically, and in the past had considered them an enemy. ECM is a form of early warning system that scans the atmosphere for electronic signals. The Russians, as well as ourselves, utilize equipment with known frequencies of energy that can be detected and traced."

"I see," Atar replied. He turned to Raval, "Take your scoutcraft and lead the others to a point that will intercept these Russians. Do whatever is necessary to defend the island and to bring their nominal leader before the council." Raval gave a silent nod then departed.

The secretary interrupted Atar and asked, "What do you intend to do?"

"Why, invite these Russians to our island to discuss trade and exchange of knowledge," Atar said quite casually, "just as I have with you."

"But-but I thought you wanted to do trade with us," stammered the secretary.

"We do, but we do not recognize your petty squabble with any other government. We never agreed to exclusive trade with you. What we have we will share with all peoples of this world. Disease is no respecter of culture or boundaries. Why then should the cure? To do so would be *barbaric*," Atar remarked, emphasizing the word barbaric.

The secretary thought for a moment then shook his head grimly. "Be careful. The Russians have been known to be ruthless. You can't trust them."

"We will take your warning under advisement," Atar replied with that familiar, all-knowing, half grin on his face.

"We must go now. With your permission, I will return later with the volunteers to donate blood," the secretary stated.

"Very well, Mord will escort you out of the city."

The large group of men was taken to the waterfront where a submersible, like the one that had brought them there, awaited to return them to their nearby ship.

Moments after everyone was aboard the *USS Lavan*, the scoutcraft submerged and silently departed. The captain went to the bridge and ordered general quarters while the wildcatters were deposited in the galley. "What's going on? Are we at war?" Paul asked loudly.

"No, Paul. The Russians are on their way to this spot, and the captain is preparing for anything," Tom answered. "I overheard a sailor tell the captain they were near."

"Then why did they take us aboard?" Paul asked again.

"They're going to take us back to the rig, shortly. They want to be ready just in case the Russians try something stupid. We are now working on trade agreements with the Atlantians," Tom explained.

"You're kidding!"

"Nope."

"After what they did. Kidnapping us!"

"Yup."

"Shit! What's this world coming to?"

The Russian cruiser was approaching the intercept point set by Atar. When it reached that spot, Raval instructed one of its two screws be disabled. An Aquarian with the maser did just that, causing the cruiser to lurch to starboard and reduce its speed suddenly. The Russians were stunned. Its commanding officer ordered, "All stop!" When the second screw ceased rotating, Raval commanded six of the scoutcraft to surface and cut down one of the cruiser's upper masts to get their attention. The instant this was accomplished, Raval's craft surfaced and he and his two crewmen stepped out into the open. Speaking fluent Russian, Raval requested to talk with the commander of the vessel. When its captain came out onto the bridge wing to speak with these strangers, he had men on either side of him with AK-47 machine rifles cocked and ready to fire. The two armed guards pointed them down at those on the submersible.

Once more in Russian, Raval called to the armed men, "Please put away your weapons. It is not in our best interest to have them aimed at us." The two men beside their captain leveled their guns. Sighting along the barrels, the men made no move to rid themselves of their weapons.

One of the accompanying Atlantians seemed to be staring at the men on the bridge wing, perhaps waiting. A moment later, he inclined his head slightly. Both of the men with the machine guns became rigid and snorted. Before one could uncock his rifle his trigger finger reflexively tightened, discharging his weapon into the water just inches in front of the submersible. By now his counterpart had lowered his gun and tossed it into the ocean. The one that had fired only now followed suit with a bewildered captain staring in total disbelief. The startled captain turned to the man on his left side and cursed at him. His tirade was cut short by another announcement from Raval.

"We do not wish conflict. We do not desire to have combat with you." Raval stopped speaking for a moment and turned to the man on his right. After a time, he returned his attention to the men on the bridge wing.

"Captain, you will please now come aboard our vessel," Raval demanded. "Do not be apprehensive, but please do not resist. Your executive officer is capable of commanding your ship in your absence. Your men may take this time to repair your starboard propeller. You will be returned to your ship by the time they have affected repairs. We simply wish to take you to our city on the island you were in such a great hurry to investigate."

The captain grew restless, eyeing the blue vessel and its occupants with suspicion. No way was he going to board this strange alien craft. Raval sensed the captain's consternation. After appearing to confer with his crewmen, Raval addressed the commander again. "We insist that you join us aboard. We do not wish to be required to use force, but will do so if..." Raval was cut short. Another crewman of the Russian cruiser was bringing a rifle to bear on the Atlantians. At Raval's unspoken command, his first mate released a small burst of energy from the maser within the vessel. Before the Russian could complete his aim, the front part of his barrel became liquid and disappeared. Startled, the crewman tossed the remainder of his weapon over the side.

Raval continued, "As I said, we do not wish conflict, but I must insist that you board our vessel now before you force me to order the destruction of more of your ship."

The Russian officer considered what Raval had said as well as everything he had just witnessed. Feeling that he had no other options, he turned to his executive officer and ordered him to anchor there, repair the ship's propeller, and await his return. He was to report this incident as soon as possible to their home base. The captain then turned and walked down the ship's ladder, climbing aboard the alien craft.

As his foot touched the outer surface of the blue vessel he noticed that it was not as firm as expected, more like walking on the back of a whale. He made a mental note of this and went inside. Shocked to see no visible controls, indicators, or propulsion devices, only a reduced size blue dome in the center, he touched the walls to explore his new surroundings, and concluded that whatever it was, the entire vessel was made of this same material.

Once everyone was inside, Raval submerged his craft and headed home. He ordered two of the scoutcraft to remain on station, and to report the actions of the Russians to him as they progressed.

Soon the craft was making its way through the maze to the entrance to the city's harbor. When they pulled into port, Mord was there to greet them and escort their guest to the great hall. The captain said little. His eyes roving from side to side taking in all the different shaped buildings, their design, and the civilization each represented. It was as if he had gone back in time or entered an ancient museum.

The two huge doors to the citadel opened upon their approach. Mord, Raval, and the commander entered. Here, in the great hall, the captain was allowed to wander about and to scrutinize the various tapestries, statues, and walls with illuminated pictographs while the council members assembled.

He was still very uneasy. Being a seaman for as long as he had, he knew these waters well. He knew there had been no such island here before, and now not only was there an island, but also one populated by people who were obviously wealthy, intelligent, and who possessed weapons far superior to any he knew existed. They used very silent submersible craft of a most radical design. *Who are these people? Where did they come from?* he wondered.

Before he could dwell on these thoughts much longer, Raval called to him and had him enter the council chamber. Atar stood up to greet the captain, speaking perfect Russian, and introduced himself and the other members of the council. "Welcome. I am Atar, leader of the Council of Elders and governing head of this metropolis. I suppose it was inevitable that another great political power would attempt to make contact with us. Only we were a bit unprepared by your timing. We do not wish any hostile action with any nation or people upon this planet, but we are more than adequately prepared to defend ourselves as you have undoubtedly witnessed. We only wish to share what we have with all mankind, freely—an exchange of cultures, ideas, and information. We do not desire to get involved with your petty politics. We remain, as you say, neutral."

Regaining his composure, the Russian commander asked, "Are you from outer space?"

Atar grinned at the suggestion then bluntly replied, "No. The fact is you might say we are from inner space. We are the people known to you as Atlantians. We have been living contentedly at the bottom of this vast body of water for well over two millennia.

"Two days ago, as you record time, we surfaced rather abruptly and unexpectedly. The volcano which originally created this island, then became extinct, was suddenly brought to life and it once more deposited us on the surface. We suffered some damage, but on the whole we have fared well. Now that we are among your kind once more we must learn to deal with you. That is why you have been brought here. We want to establish trade with your people, and to have them and the world recognize us as a separate government, with its own boundaries and sovereignty. We want you to respect our borders if we are to do trade with you."

"Ha, ha, ha, what do you have that my people would want?" sneered the captain.

Atar reflected and then said, "How about a cure for AIDS?"

The captain was astonished. How could these people have a cure for the world's most dreaded disease when his own country's top scientists hadn't been able to do so in fifty years. They admitted to surfacing only two days ago. In two days they learn about AIDS and cure it—impossible! "Can this be true?" asked the commander.

"I assure you that not only is this true, but we have many more accomplishments we are willing to share," Atar declared.

"May I report this to my superiors?"

Studying the commander for a moment, Atar replied, "Yes, you may. Raval, the one who brought you here, will return you to your ship. But be warned, we will only allow small envoys to enter our city. Any hostile actions toward us will result in our withdrawing any exchange of knowledge, and the complete and utter destruction of the warring faction. We are a peaceful people, but we show no mercy to our enemies."

"How then may we communicate with you?" inquired the Russian captain diplomatically.

Any vessel that enters our waters within six miles from our shores, as you measure distance, will be greeted by one of our scoutcraft. Messages and personnel shall be conveyed by them. Later we shall trade for your form of communication device and the use of our scoutcraft will no longer be necessary," Atar answered.

"As you wish," replied the officer.

Raval returned the anxious captain to his anchored ship. When they departed, Mord mentally inquired, *What now?*

In silent communication, the council members debated their next course of action.

✄❖✄

"Sir, sonar reports that the Russian's engines have stopped," the messenger of the watch informed the CO. Commander Wells mused for a moment; *Atar's men must have intercepted them.* He couldn't think of anything else that would have caused them to go dead in the water. *I hope he knows what he is doing. We don't need an international incident.* "Set the condition three underway watch," he ordered.

When the announcement came over the 1-MC, Paul asked, "What does that mean?"

Tom answered, "It's a reduced general quarters. All stations remain manned, but the ship's crew can move about the ship easier."

David Holbrook came down from the bridge and greeted the group. "Sorry I didn't come down sooner, but when GQ was sounded I decided to remain where I was, on the bridge. Is everyone alright?"

Paul spouted off in his macho way, "Yeah, we're alright. It's a good thing you came when you did, or I might have bashed in a few heads back there."

Tom interjected, "Are we on our way back to the rig?"

"Yes, the captain ordered a course change and we should be at the rig within the hour," David responded.

In the wardroom the engineer addressed the Secretary of State. "First things first. We'll return these men to their rig, and then we'll come back to the island. In the meantime we'll locate three volunteers to donate blood for you."

"Very well," replied the secretary. "Has my report been sent to Washington?"

"Yes sir, it has," answered the communications officer.

Arthur felt reinvigorated. This would be quite a feather in his cap when he returned with the cure to AIDS. All he needed now was an AIDS victim.

In Washington D.C. the secretary's report was being passed around until it finally landed on the president's desk. After reading the report, the president called for the press secretary. Upon his arrival the president expressed, "I want a press conference. Mr. Franks has discovered the lost city of Atlantis and its inhabitants. They have surfaced and hold the key to the cure for AIDS. We will need to find a volunteer to donate blood and to test the new serum out."

"You're not serious? Atlantis! A cure for AIDS! Come on, surely Mr. Franks has been drinking," stated the press secretary.

"I'm positive he is sober and of sound judgment. Commander Wells of the *USS Lavan* supports his report. Now arrange that press conference. Time is of the essence."

Within the hour the president entered the pressroom to make his announcement. When all persons quieted in the room he began his speech. "A short while ago I received a message from Secretary of State Franks. Earlier he had been sent out on a mission to acquire the release of some workers from one of our oil rigs in the Atlantic held hostage by a group of unknown origin. Upon his arrival to the scene he discovered that their captors were not a terrorist group, but in fact inhabitants of the once, thought to be lost, fabled island of Atlantis." An uproar occurred throughout the room at the uttering of the word *Atlantis*.

"Mr. President! Mr. President!" shouted many of the news personnel raising their hands to get his attention.

The president pointed to a woman in the front row. "Mrs. Janet Jean of the Washington Post."

"This has been confirmed? Atlantis, that is?" Mrs. Jean asked in her excitement.

"Commander Wells, captain of the destroyer *USS Lavan* has sent confirmation," he replied.

"Mr. President! Mr. President!" called the frantic news personnel, once more vying for his attention.

Pointing to a man in the right rear of the pressroom, the president announced, "Mr. Donald Carnicom of the New York Times."

"Mr. President, are there any details as to what they look like?" Mr. Carnicom asked.

"No details of that nature have been sent, as of yet," answered the president in a calm voice.

Another shout for attention and the president selected another woman; this time in the center row. "Ms. Stephanie Reynolds of the Chicago Tribune."

"Rumor has it that these Atlantians have developed a cure for cancer. Is that true?" she asked.

"I don't know about cancer, but they do claim they can produce a cure for AIDS." A rumble spread around the pressroom as each news person murmured their astonishment. "They have indicated that all they lack is a blood sample from an AIDS victim; one willing to test the new serum. That is why I have called this press conference. We need someone afflicted with the disease willing to donate blood and to try this new serum, and we need that person here as soon as possible. We have a helicopter waiting to take that individual to the Atlantian's island, so alert your various media. Time is critical." The president then ended the press conference. "Thank you for your time."

As the president turned from the podium to depart, the press secretary announced, "All rise," and as a show of respect, all the news personnel stood as the president departed the pressroom.

On television and in the newspapers the president's message was sent out. Within a few hours of the press conference, the news media and press secretary were swamped with calls, emails, and twitter messages from frantic volunteers. A local man in the Washington D.C. area was selected; mainly because he was so close by. His name was withheld to protect his job and family, so he was known only by his first name and last initial—Mr. Henry D.

As soon as he could arrange to be at the airport, he was flown out on one of the president's personal helicopters to the *USS Lavan* and greeted by Mr. Franks and Commander Wells. The *USS Lavan* had only an hour before returned the wildcatters to their oil rig. These men would be busy for the next month affecting repairs to their rig.

As the ship came to a spot six miles from the Atlantian's coastline a large blue object surfaced silently beside them. One man appeared on its surface calling to the lookout who announced the arrival of the, now familiar, Atlantian craft. Commander Wells came to the bridge wing to talk to the Atlantian. It was Raval.

"Atar thought it best if you were greeted by a familiar face," Raval called out to the captain.

"Tell Atar thank you and that we appreciate the gesture. Do you wish to come aboard?" the captain inquired.

"No. I have come for those men your secretary had promised would volunteer."

"Please give us some time to brief the men, and to have them gather some personal belongings."

"Very well, I must, however, request that your ship approach no closer to our island."

"As you wish; I have no problem with that." Turning toward the bridge the commander gave the orders to the helm and navigator to comply with Raval's request. Turning back to face the stalwart Atlantian, Commander Wells noticed that he was gone. No big blue bubble; nothing was in sight. He shrugged and returned to his seat on the bridge. Getting the messenger's attention, he said, "Inform Mr. Franks that Raval is waiting for his volunteers, and bring me back a cup of coffee."

While the messenger repeated the captain's order, Commander Wells handed him his cup. As he ended his recitation with a hearty, "Aye sir!" the seaman grabbed the cup and left to carry out his duties.

CHAPTER TWELVE

A fter one hour had passed, the familiar blue craft surfaced alongside the *USS Lavan*. The lookout informed the captain at once, as
he was prepared for their arrival. Word was also sent to the secretary
and his volunteers.

The group assembled near the accommodation ladder where
Raval had maneuvered his craft into position. Before long they were
on their way to the island. Henry was very excited. Not only was
he going to visit the legendary Atlantis, but they were going to cure
him of this heartrending disease. The craft also excited him. It was
so strange, so unique. In a short time the submersible had made its
way through the maze and into the city's harbor. This time they were
greeted by a woman with raven hair and a fat, balding old man, who
didn't say much when they arrived. The woman introduced herself as
Rhonda and instructed them to follow her to the life science building.
Once inside she continued walking toward the rear of the building,
taking the group to a room which had all the walls brightly illuminated. This area appeared like any run-of-the-mill doctor's examining
room with four separate padded tables. Before the secretary could
enter, Rhonda stopped him, "I'm sorry, but I can't allow you in. This
is our sterile room. Only those actually involved may go in. Besides,
this process is going to take much time, it would bore you, and your
presence is not required. Atar has invited you to the citadel to discuss
trade agreements. Nena, my assistant, will escort you to the citadel."
Disappointed, he agreed and left with Nena.

Following the men into the sterile room, Rhonda explained the
procedures to them, "During the next few time intervals I will do
some standard comparative checks of your vital organs and muscle

tone. Later, I will take samples of all your body fluids. We will test and compare these. Finally we will give each of you a full body exam comparing appendage movement and radius, reflex, strength, and dexterity. When this is done we will break for a rest period then in the morning, as you call it, we will continue. At that time we will check and compare endurance and changes in your biochemistry to different types of stress. Concluding our biodynamics testing we will then give you a break until the next day. Again, in the morning I will take samples of your blood, and by the morrow I should have a usable serum prepared." She turned to face the AIDS victim. "Henry, you will have to stay in our isolation suite."

"I understand," was all the reply he could make. Henry accepted the fact that he would have to be isolated from the others. He had experienced such isolation first hand. Ever since he acknowledged he had this terrible disease he was shunned. His wife threw him out of his house. It was all he could do to hide this information from his employer. Now maybe there was a chance he could get cured. If so, he would be the first.

"Now let us get started, each one of you on a table. Henry, you're at the end. Each of you disrobe and put these on." Rhonda then handed each of them a short garment similar to a loin cloth, only a little less revealing. John, one of the volunteers from the Navy needed some assistance getting his fastened. She then gave each man a pair of soft sandals.

Calling in another of her assistants from a nearby room, she had the men's clothing gathered. "Your clothes will be returned to you when we have finished. Until then you will dress like one of us." As the assistant departed, Rhonda started her examinations. "Before we get too far along I will have to secure this room and sterilize it and ourselves. This process can cause damage to your optic nerve, so you must wear these protective devices. They will safeguard your eyes during the sterilization phase." She handed each man a pair of goggles that looked like they were made from the bottom of old Coke bottles. The one noticeable difference is that they seemed to refract light like some finely cut crystal or diamonds. Once each of them had their glasses in place, Rhonda closed the door and walked over to a table. Her hand came over what appeared to be a multicolored, multifaceted glass ball; as she did so she explained what was about to happen. "The walls, ceiling, and floor will glow brighter, change colors, and then return to white. When the room returns to a white glow I will then indicate when it is safe for you to remove your protective eye gear." Rhonda turned to face this unusual glass control knob. The room filled with a light blue color that became deeper and richer in hue. It then changed to violet, followed by red, where it lingered a moment before continuing to run the spectrum, finally concluding with white.

Each man held his breath throughout the process. When the room returned to white Rhonda turned to face them and said, "You may now remove your eyewear. The room is once more sterile."

"What was that all about?" asked John.

"The spectrum of light you saw was a form of irradiation. It kills all microorganisms in the air and on our bodies." She then walked up to John who was on the first table. Taking what appeared to be a stethoscope from the table she began to poke and prod in the usual manner done by physicians. She listened intently to his heart and lungs. When finished she placed the device she was using back on the table and picked up a round white object about the size of a baseball. "Which hand is your strongest?" she asked him.

"My right," John replied.

Rhonda placed the white object in his right hand. Upon closer inspection he noticed that this was some sort of stone. It was porous and reminded him of pumice, volcanic glass. "Squeeze with all your might. Squeeze this stone with only your right hand," she instructed him. The others just watched. As he squeezed, some of the porous mineral wore away. His hand turned red and white as he pressed into the object.

With his hand tired and throbbing he gave the stone back to Rhonda. "Very good," she said in a condescending tone. As he handed the stone to her he noticed that his hand had left an impression in it.

"What was that for?" John asked.

"It's a test of physical strength and muscle tone. We measure the depth of the marks your fingers made while compressing the stone, and compare it to those of our race during their course of development."

"Well, how do I compare?" John asked defensively, feeling his macho image in danger.

"Adequate," Rhonda simply replied.

John was getting exasperated. "Listen lady, I bench press 250 pounds. I'm no weakling!"

"I'm sorry if I offended you. You are the first surface dwellers we have come in contact with in over two millennia," Rhonda explained. "Haven't you guessed that our physic is different? All those years living at the bottom of this vast body of water, the greater pressure we endured, the greater gravitational pull, all this has had an effect on us. It is now inherent in our life string. What you call genes."

"No, I didn't think. You look so normal to me," replied John, "and beautiful."

"Why thank you."

She walked over to the next man on the table and commenced to do the same examination. After she finished with Henry, she announced, "Now it's time to take samples of your body fluids; first your tears and saliva." She went up to John and took two different colored glass tubes from the nearby table. "I'm going to cover one of your eyes with my hand, and using this tube I will place it near your tear duct and allow your tears to fill it. There is no pain to this. All you have to do is remain still for a moment," Rhonda reassured. After she collected his tears she said, "See, that didn't hurt. Now open your mouth." John did, and in a similar manner she collected a sample of his saliva.

John was wondering if this collection of body fluids included semen, and if so, how was she going to collect it? This thought both embarrassed and excited him.

Rhonda concluded her collection of tears and saliva and then prepared to collect blood. First she swabbed a cool, colorless liquid over their arms. "This will make it so you will feel no pain. All you will feel is coolness." After that, to their surprise, collecting their blood samples was done in the same manner as the men were used to.

John watched her closely. She was right. He didn't feel a thing. He wished it was this easy back home. She finished collecting the blood samples. Finally the moment of truth!

"Now I will need to collect samples of your semen," Rhonda said flatly.

"Where do you want us to go to prepare to get you the sample?" remarked John.

"There is no need for that. I know of a technique that will get me the samples I require," she said.

John looked at her in surprise, mentally guessing, *Fellatio?*

She then knelt down in front of John and said, "You first." His thoughts raced as she pulled up his tunic to reveal his manhood. He was ridged with excitement. Placing a small glass cup near the end of his penis, she placed her other hand between his thighs. Pressing a finger into a pressure spot just behind his testicles, it caused him to ejaculate. She pressed three more times and collected, what she thought was enough. John went limp again from disappointment. "Now that wasn't too bad, was it?" asked Rhonda.

In a professional manner she did the same to the other three men. None of whom could figure out just how she managed that. Speaking to the group as a whole, Rhonda declared, "See, not too bad after all, was it?"

The men remained silent. "Alright then, time for the final examination for the day." She went to the table and picked up an instrument that looked like a large compass. Turning to face John she explained to the group, "I am going to measure the angular displacement that you can achieve with your appendages in all planes." She then set about measuring the degrees of free movement each man could achieve raising his arms forward, backward, and out to the side. The same was done with the legs and even each finger and thumb. Finally, with their legs about shoulder width apart, she had them twist their torso to the extreme right and then to the extreme left, and then forward and back. She paid particular attention to the curve of each man's spine.

"Very well, I have enough information to get me started. We will do the reflex and dexterity tests tomorrow, along with the endurance and stress tests. That will be all for today. My assistant will take you to the citadel where guest rooms have been prepared for you." Picking up some neatly folded, satiny, blue material that was lying on a table near the entrance, she gave each a bundle. "You may feel better with more covering. As I said earlier, for the next few days you will dress like one of us, and this is the outer garment worn by the males of my race."

John stared. A toga! Boy, did this bring back memories.

Turning to Henry, Rhonda said comfortingly, "Rest assured, Henry. I will have that cure for you within four of your days."

Henry humbly replied, "Thank you."

In the morning the group was awakened, fed, and escorted back to the life science building. Rhonda and Henry were there waiting for them. Instead of going to the sterile room she led them to a small chamber. Inside was a giant of a man. He sported a beard and had thick, black, coarse hair covering his chest and back. He stood there and just smiled.

"This is Emrah. He is a Soschatch," Rhonda said. "They are the ones who build and repair our city's buildings. Today he is going to help me do comparative studies on your dexterity, endurance, reflex, and stress. This test will take most of the day. In this test you may either work as a team or separately. This I will leave up to you. Since it will take most of the day, you will be provided with food and drink in pouches for you to carry. Momentarily, we will go to the labyrinth. These are our proving grounds. Events are held here to entertain the populous. I think you call them *sports*."

Rhonda then brought the group to a table. On it was a multi-colored, multifaceted crystalline sphere with edges that looked like quartz. "In the center of the labyrinth is a crystal sphere similar to this one. Touch it once and the center room seals itself off from the remainder of the labyrinth. In the span of time you call three minutes, you must touch it again. This second touch will cause the door to open to a passageway that will return you to this room. I will be waiting for you to take a sample of your breath, blood, and measure once more your strength. When I have done this we will be finished for the day and you may then rest or roam about the city freely."

"That sounds all well and good, but what is a labyrinth?" asked John.

Answering John, Henry explained, "A labyrinth is a maze. According to mythology, King Minos of Crete had some guy named Daedalus build this vast maze to house the Minotaur. Later some guy named Theseus killed the Minotaur."

"That's awful!" cried Rhonda.

"It's only a myth, a legend."

"Little does your kind know," stated Rhonda bluntly, and refused to discuss it any further.

"What must we do in this labyrinth?" asked Don, one of the other naval volunteers.

Rhonda thought to herself, *survive*, but answered, "This will be like a game, but a very serious one. You could get injured if you are not quick-witted enough or if your reflexes are poor. The labyrinth itself holds its own dangers. Getting lost is the least of them. There are deep pits, tunnels, pools of water, half-height sharpened walls, and all along you will be chased by Emrah. Besides food and drink you will be given these…" She pointed to what appeared to be jai alai rackets and hard rubber balls. "The object of this exercise is to reach the center first and press the controller twice. This must be done before Emrah has a chance to hit you with one of his balls. To end your participation in the game the rule is he must hit you with one ball. Once hit you are out. You forfeit your balls to Emrah and he continues to pursue the others. He is originally given only four balls, as are each of you. You or your team, however, must hit him three times in order to stop his advance. This is how each team or side is made equal. The danger is not only the labyrinth, but Emrah. His strength enables him to hurl a ball with such force as to shatter bone. I'll demonstrate." She then gave Emrah one of those stones the group tried to indent earlier which recorded their strength. Once in his hand he crushed it with ease. A discernible gasp was made by the group.

"You will be monitored each step of the way. Your advantage is speed and quick wit. He is slow, yet strong. Another thing, as you make your way into the labyrinth the panels that make up the walls, ceiling, and floor will illuminate when there is pressure applied to the floor, as well as the forward adjacent sections, as you traverse. Once all pressure is removed the section goes dark again. In this manner your presence will be either hid or displayed to your opponent depending on how close you get to one another. Do you have any questions before you start?"

"You implied we can use a hurtled ball as ammunition back at our friend there?" John inquired as he pointed to Emrah.

"Yes, which is why the rackets are in the shape they are. One can catch with the racket and use it to shoot back at his opponent," she explained.

"Henry then asked, "Any suggestions?"

"Yes, the labyrinth is full of items like ropes, polls, and such. These may be gathered to aid you through the obstacles. But be warned, if you collect too many objects it may hamper your progress and slow you down. This will only result in giving Emrah time to catch up with you. As it is, you will be given only a ten minute head start, as you record time." Pausing only a moment she declared, "There is no more time to discuss this. You must gather your things and go."

The group quickly gathered their pouches of food, water, and four hard balls each, as well as the rackets. Then Rhonda took them through a downward sloping passage to the entrance of the labyrinth. It was like they were going into a subway. Arriving at their destination, they saw that only the entrance to the labyrinth was illuminated. Beyond that point it was a dark tunnel. "Your time starts now," announced Rhonda.

The group made their way rapidly along the winding corridor until they reached the first junction. The panels illuminated ahead of them as Rhonda had earlier described, but not far enough to determine if there was a dead end or not.

"She said that as long as there was pressure on the floor this section and the next would light, right?" John asked rhetorically. "Henry, you go right. Don, you go left. Jason, you go straight ahead. I'll stay here. Go as far as it takes for the panels behind you to go out, and no further. Check if you can see if there is a dead end, then return. We'll decide at that point which direction to go," John instructed, taking charge of the group with his authoritative commands. Each man returned with the same reply. They didn't see any dead end.

Henry spoke up, "I remember one of my math teachers telling me once that if you put your hand on one wall you will always find the center of a maze. It may take a little longer, but you will always find the center."

"How is that?" asked John.

Henry explained as he drew a pattern with his racket on the floor. "You see, even if you come to a dead end you follow it back to the passage that sent you there and you continue on. In that way you are bound to find the doorway into the center." The others shook their heads in understanding, and then Henry continued. "All we need to do now is pick a direction."

John suggested, "Let's go left then. It won't be much longer till that giant comes after us, and if we are far enough down a corridor he won't know what direction we took."

"Good idea. Let's go," exclaimed Henry.

It wasn't long before the group came to their first obstacle, an eight-foot wall. The summit was covered with shards of sharp crystal. "How do we get over that?" asked Henry.

They were silent, and then John came up with an idea. "Jason, here, gather up the food from my pouch and Don's. These pouches appear to be made of some kind of leather, and I will probably be able to use them to protect myself from the shards as I climb over. Don, you and Henry boost me up to the top. I'll drape the pouches over the shards and climb over."

"That's all well and good for you, but how do we get over after you?" inquired Jason.

"The two of you can help push Henry over, and then toss the food and water pouches over to us. We can then tie our tunics together to make a sort of rope, and help pull each of you over, one at a time," explained John.

"Alright, I guess that will work," said Jason seeing John's logic.

"Hurry, I don't think we have much time!" John hissed. "Quick, give me the pouches and boost me up!" Don and Henry did just that. It seemed like an eternity holding John in place while he set the pouches on the shards of crystal. "This one feels loose. I'll pull it out. That will get it out of our way, and who knows we might be able to use it later."

"Quit babbling!" yelled Henry. "Just hurry and get yourself over. You're no featherweight you know!" John's foot was digging into his shoulder.

After he got himself over, John said, "OK, your turn Henry." Jason and Don boosted the only civilian of the group over the wall. Once on the other side of the wall Henry cried out, "Wait a minute. I think I see something." He walked a little bit down the corridor and returned triumphantly with a coil of rope.

"What's the hold-up?" Jason yelled.

"Hold your horses, will ya," remarked John. "Henry's found some rope. I'll toss it over to you, and we'll pull you over," John shouted back.

The few minutes seemed like an eternity. Finally John, Don, and Henry pulled Jason over the wall. "Can we rest a minute, now?" asked Jason.

"You can if you want, but I don't want to be here when that giant comes over that wall," Henry replied, pushing one of the hard balls in Jason's face. "You saw what he did to that stone. Do you really want one of these *balls* shot against your body?" Jason didn't bother to reply. He just went about gathering his food pouch and other possessions. John slipped the sharp crystal shard into his food pouch while Henry grabbed the rope. The group was on their way once again. They didn't exactly run, but they sure walked very fast. They continued down the path until they came to another junction, this time the choice was to go left again or to continue on straight ahead.

"Well, like the man said, pick a wall and stick to it," John said flatly, "we've been keeping left, so I guess that's the way we'll go now." The others just nodded their heads in approval.

Taking the left junction they quickly made their way down its corridor about two hundred feet and almost ran into the solid wall in front of them. "Now what?" asked Henry.

"Turn around and go back to the junction that led us here, I guess. Then we can make another left, and continue down the corridor we were originally in," remarked John.

The group retraced their steps back to the junction and turned left. It wasn't fifteen feet further when John, who was in the lead, stepped on the next floor panel, and a wall section dropped down in front of them blocking their way. "Shit!" exclaimed Don. "Now what do we do?"

Before anyone could answer him, Emrah, the giant, came into view. He took a ball from his small pouch he had tied to his waist, and placed it into his racket. With a low grunt he hurled his ball at John. John was quick to react, catching the ball in his racket he whirled it back at the giant. Emrah caught it and flung it back at him. This time John ducked, and the ball crashed against the newly positioned wall segment striking a hidden trip switch which caused the wall section to raise about eighteen inches. John and the others were amazed. John urged, "Crawl through! I'll hold him off."

His companions fell to the floor and quickly started to crawl through the narrow gap. In seconds Emrah had retrieved his fallen projectile and hurled it down toward the escaping men. John barely caught it with the tip of his racket as the momentum of the ball carried his arm backward. Flinging the ball back at the giant with all his might, John missed, and the ball ricocheted off the corridor wall. The giant lumbered back, and with his long, outstretched arm caught the ricocheted ball with his racket, and aligned himself for another throw. By now the other three had made their way under and past the precarious wall section. The giant made another mighty throw, and John caught it with agility and returned it his way. "Come on, John!" came a plaintive plea from the other side of the wall.

Then Henry yelled a suggestion, "Keep the next ball he throws, John. That way he will have less ammunition to hurl at us. We can win simply by his being unable to stop us with his balls."

John heard and understood Henry's meaning. On the giant's next throw John kept the shot, and dropped to the floor. Emrah saw what John was trying to do, and hastened to place another ball into his racket. As John was scurrying through the narrow gap under the wall section, his companions took hold of his arm to pull him through. The giant threw his next ball. He was so angered by his past performance that his aim was off in his haste and it struck the wall just over John's head. As it hit the section it tripped another hidden switch. This time the wall section closed again. Fortunately, John's companions were able to pull him through before the section came crashing down.

Returning to his feet John exclaimed, "Let's get out of here! That giant looked mighty pissed off, and I don't want to be here when he figures out a way through this wall."

On the other side of the wall a very angry Emrah pounded his fists against the barrier in front of him. Not known for their patience, like others of his kind, the giant turned and walked back down the corridor retracing his steps to a junction he had passed earlier. There he turned and went to locate the center of the labyrinth by going in that direction.

The group again quickly made their way down the corridor. Cautious at first, they slowly picked up their momentum to a fast walk. Continuing in this direction they made their way to yet another obstacle. Jason was the first to come upon the pools—two pools of liquid separated only by a narrow, low partition. Jason first tested this unknown liquid by placing his racket into it. When nothing happened he thought that the substance must be safe to touch. As he reached toward the liquid he could sense great heat, and noticed whiffs of steam coming from it. With determination, and great effort, he forced his hand into the liquid. "Damn!" he shouted as he pulled his hand from the water, and shook it in the air. "That shit's hot!"

"What is it?" asked Don.

"Scalding hot water," replied Jason, still shaking his hand in the air.

John knelt over and inspected the hot water. He put his hand in to test it, then remarked, "I've been in hot tubs in Japan with water as hot as this. I think we can swim across to the other side as long as we don't spend too long in it. Here, take these." John handed Henry his food and water pouches. "I'll go first." As he spoke these words he lowered himself into the steaming hot water. Every nerve ending was tingling as he did so, and he screamed out in agony. He finally touched bottom, his neck and head were the only appendages above the water line. Soon his nerve endings quieted down, and all that remained was the heat that soaked into his body. With effort on his part he grinned and said, "See, piece of cake." He then began to swim to the other side. It was a swim of about twelve feet. He then climbed on top the narrow partition. Up until now all eyes were upon him, every mouth shut. You could hear a pin drop. "See I told you, a piece of cake."

"What's the next pool like?" Henry asked.

"How should I know?" John yelled back indignantly. Turning around he put his hand into the next pool. At first he sensed heat, next his senses detected extreme cold. "Shit, this one is freezing!" Before anyone could say another word, John slid into the adjacent pool of icy water. As he did so he hissed a long drawn-out, "Ssshhhiitttt!"

John managed to swim rapidly to the other side, shaking, teeth chattering—he climbed out of the pool. As his foot made contact with the floor, the dark section near that end of the pool illuminated. There, masked in the darkness, were several towels waiting for them as if they were expected. John grabbed one of the towels and dried himself off. He then called out to the others, "Toss me the pouches."

They quickly did as he instructed. Soon, one after the other, they started across this next obstacle. After reaching the other side they all dried off, and everyone was quite amazed at how rapidly their tunics dried, seemingly by themselves, as if they shed water. Don remarked, "Some kind of neat material. My outfit is completely dry."

"Mine too," Jason added.

"Well, let's get this over with," stated John, their nominal leader. As he started down the corridor he called back, "Come on. Let's go!"

The others wearily followed behind him. They continued until they came upon a Y-shaped crossing. It was here that Jason suggested, "You guys continue toward the left. I'll take the right fork and see where it reaches. That woman, Rhonda, did say we could go our separate ways."

"I don't know. I think that we should stay together," remarked Henry.

"Oh, go ahead. Let him go," Don injected.

"You two stop your bickering," ordered John. "Jason, go ahead and go that way. Who's to say which way is right. We're going to keep left. It's gotten us this far," exclaimed John. Jason went right, and the others went left. It wasn't long before the group came upon the next obstacle. John was leading the way, as usual, and when he stepped on the floor panel just forty feet from the fork where the group separated the section lit up, but so did a web of what appeared to be red laser light. This time they seemed to be stumped. They didn't know what to do.

First Don stuck his racket into the intersecting laser beams. It was cut in two and part of it burst into flame. "Ooohhh boy!" shouted Don. "Any suggestions? Maybe we should go back."

They all stopped and thought a while. Then John had an inspiration. He reached into his food pouch and pulled out the sharp crystal shard. He examined it a minute, wondering, then turned to face the others and asked, "Do you think this crystal could be used like a prism?" He showed them the shard he had collected earlier.

"What do you mean—like a prism?" inquired Henry.

"You know. A prism can refract light. Do you think that this crystal can bend the light as well?" John asked.

"Well, I guess so. Why?" Henry replied.

"Well, a laser beam is a concentration of light. If this crystal can refract light it might be able to disperse this laser," John explained.

"I just don't know," replied Henry. "I guess it's worth a try."

"OK, you guys step back. Just in case," suggested John. John then placed the sharp crystal shard into one of the intersecting laser beams that made up this web of deadly light. To his and his companions' surprise, the light didn't refract, but bent away from its aimed course.

When he did so, parts of the web disappeared, the light no longer striking some of the reflective panels.

"That's what's been bothering me!" Henry shouted with excitement. "A prism refracts light, or bends it. It refracts white light because white light is many colors or frequencies of light blended together. This red laser light is only one color, one frequency, so it bends."

John appeared to ignore what Henry was telling him. He was engrossed in the task at hand. He simply followed the path of the laser light, bending it away from himself, up to its source. Steadily holding the crystal in place, he said, "Come on. Hurry and get through here. My arm's getting tired."

Henry and Don grabbed their possessions, and quickly made their way past John. John cautiously aimed the deadly, red laser beam away from himself as he made his way to the other side of the webbed barricade. Once on the other side, he removed the crystal, and the deadly laser web took shape once more.

As the trio continued on down the corridor the floor began to incline. It soon became an incline of about twenty-five degrees. Henry was getting exhausted, and stopped. "Please! Let's take a moment to rest. I'm pooped!"

"We've got to keep going. That giant could be right behind us," stated John. "He could catch up with us at any minute. We've got to keep moving." Turning to face Don he said, "Don, help me with Henry."

Don and John helped Henry up the steep incline and soon it leveled off. Another section passed by, and then the passage became a steep decline. Now they were almost running down the steep declining corridor. This, too, changed to a level spot, and then changed again to another incline. This incline was closer to thirty-five degrees. The trio trudged along until they reached the next summit. There the corridor flattened out.

Jason continued on down the fork he chose to explore. He passed by another junction that connected from the right. This corridor appeared to be free of obstacles until it made a ninety degree bend to the left. Once he rounded the corner he saw it—a large pit. Jason stopped in his tracks the moment he saw it. He quickly turned around in time to see Emrah emerge from the adjacent corridor. Jason took a fleeting glance over his shoulder at the pit behind him. Returning his attention to Emrah he noticed the Soschatch placing a ball into his racket. Without a moment's hesitation Jason's decision was made. His muscles rippled as they reacted to the commanding thoughts of his decision, and suddenly his body sprang into action. With a mighty running leap that strained at his muscles, Jason turned and attempted to jump the wide gap that formed the pit. As he leapt Emrah hurled his ball at Jason's back.

Jason didn't make it to the other side, his body slamming against the pit's far wall, fingers scrambling to grab a handhold on the rim, his weight pulling him down into the deep chasm. Emrah's ball flew over Jason's head as he fell into the pit.

When Jason's feet touched the bottom of the hole he spun his body around, looking up to see Emrah's sneering face. Jason hadn't caught his breath from the wind that was knocked out of him when slamming against the wall. Emrah hurled his second ball at him.

Jason's adrenalin was flowing. His reactions quickened. Grabbing his racket he deflected Emrah's incoming ball.

Undaunted, Emrah took his third ball and flung it toward Jason. Jason couldn't get his racket up in time, so he ducked his head to dodge the incoming projectile.

The ball caromed off the wall, striking a hidden switch, and ricocheted back toward Emrah where it embedded itself just below the lip of the pit. A series of louvers near the mouth of the pit opened and sand began to leak from them. Sand that began to fill the pit, sand that clung and sucked at Jason's feet, making it almost impossible to move.

The sand was going to bury, to smother, and to suffocate its unwitting captive. Jason struggled with great difficulty trying to climb or swim through the shifting sand under his feet. His legs were now buried in the stuff, his mind reeling as his only thought was escape. He began to panic. Struggling futilely, he was going to be buried unless he got out of there soon. He was going to die!

He continued to struggle and pull at his legs, which were being sucked down with every motion he made. Emrah reached down and, pulling the stuck ball out of the wall with ease, returned it to his pouch and stood there watching Jason's struggle. Finally Jason was starting to make progress as he pulled each leg out and began to crawl on his hands and knees. The sand soon filled the pit enough for Jason to crawl out from the far side of the pit. Wheezing, trying to catch his breath from all his expended energy, Jason pulled himself and rolled over into a sitting position. Emrah then removed his last ball from his leather pouch and placed it into his racket. This was going to be his last chance at scoring a hit on one of the surface dwellers.

Emrah took careful aim as Jason looked at him through the corner of his eye. When Emrah drew back his arm to fling the missile, Jason rolled and turned, placing his racket between him and the giant.

Emrah followed through with his throw. This time Jason was able to catch it. Jason then debated for a moment whether to hurl it back at Emrah or not. Reaching a decision, Jason tossed the ball into the still filling pit, allowing the ball to be buried. That's one less ball he'd have to use against him. Jason wearily dragged himself to his feet, and forced himself to walk quickly down the corridor, leaving Emrah and the pit behind.

The trio finally made their way into the heart of the labyrinth. As John's foot touched the floor of the chamber, it illuminated. In the center, on a pedestal, was the long-sought-after prize, the multifaceted crystal ball. Noticing that everyone had made it inside the room, John touched the crystalline sphere. The doorway they had entered slid shut behind them but nothing else happened. "Now what?" came a furious shout from John.

Henry answered him with a question, "Don't you remember what Rhonda said? To open the entrance where she is waiting we have to touch it again."

"Oh yeah," replied John, hitting his head with his right hand. He then touched the glowing, brightly colored sphere once more, and a panel slid open.

John and Don helped Henry through the door, then collapsed. They had survived their ordeal. Rhonda rushed up to the heavily-breathing men and asked each to blow into the bottle she had handed each of them. Next she took some blood samples, but this time only a small amount, one vial apiece. Finally she gave each that familiar white stone and recorded their strength level now, while they were still under stress. "If I knew it was going to be like that, I never would have volunteered," stated John as he caught his breath.

The last member of the group crawled through the door exhausted. Rhonda quickly had him blow into a bottle and took some blood also. "Gawd! Am I alive?" he asked between wheezes. "Whew, am I glad that's over!"

"Rest," Rhonda said comfortingly, "you deserve it. Now you may go about wherever you wish. Alice, my assistant, will attend to your needs. I must process these quickly if the results are to be accurate." Rhonda turned and left the room. Behind her she left a very beautiful girl with long blonde hair, who had a smile that could melt your heart.

Turning to face Henry, John said, "I hope you appreciate this. You know the only reason we're doing this is to help you and those afflicted with your disease." John was careful not to say the word AIDS.

"I am," replied Henry, "and to show it I'll buy you a drink at the next bar we get to."

"Drink? What kind of drink do you wish to have?" Alice inquired with a smile.

"I doubt if you have the kind of drink I'm thinking of," remarked Henry.

"Oh, I wouldn't be so quick to judge," John injected. "I was with the first landing party, and I had a chance to try some of their drink. God is it some potent shit! Three of my shipmates are still comatose, and I could have sworn I made love to a mermaid."

"You're kidding?" said Henry in amazement.

"Nope, but I don't know what it's called to ask for it again, nor where it was we found it, but it was somewhere in this city," answered John.

Alice handed each a cold towel, and they used them to wipe off their brows and to cool off their hot perspiring bodies. "If you are speaking of the public house I know where to go," Alice said innocently.

"Well, lead on," John said, as he looked about himself at the other bedraggled men.

They stood up following Alice. Henry said, "I don't think I'm allowed to go."

Alice replied, "Our preliminary tests show your disease is not airborne, and as long as you use the same goblet there is little chance you could infect anyone else. Rhonda has told me that as long as you keep that in mind you may enjoy the city as well."

For the first time in ages Henry smiled a broad smile and said to the group, "Well, what's keeping us? Let's party!"

When they were awakened the next morning, none of them could figure out how they got back to their rooms. The night before was a blank. In fact, they remembered little of the entire day before. The ordeal of the labyrinth was missing from their minds, only the fact that they entered and sometime later exited remained.

After bathing, they were escorted to the, now familiar, life science building. Rhonda was waiting for them, and so was a short, fat, balding old man.

"Who is that?" asked John aloud as they approached the building.

"He is Oman, the creator of destinies," their escort answered mysteriously.

Once inside the building, Rhonda gave each of them a glass of dark green liquid. It appeared similar to the stuff they were drinking the night before. "Here, take this and drink it," instructed Rhonda.

At first it tasted like tangerine, and then it soured like grapefruit, and finally metamorphosed once more to an orange juice taste as they gulped down this strange concoction.

"Now what?" asked Don.

"Shhhh!" ordered Rhonda, placing a finger to her lips. Keeping her eye on the group she nodded rhythmically: *four, three, two, one.* As the thought *one* crossed her mind each man collapsed to the floor unconscious.

Turning to Oman in her mind she heard him say: *We will know momentarily if the serum works. When they recover consciousness wait a moment, and then take their blood sample one last time. I'll do the final comparison, and verify that the disease is no more, and that the others now have the new Tau cell complex. I'll wait for you in the laboratory.* Oman then left the group heaped on the floor.

Rhonda shook her head. She did so hope this would work. She felt Henry's despair, and the others' fear.

In about ten minutes the men began to stir. "Wha—what happened?" the first to wake up asked.

"I don't think you liked your drink," she answered, amused, as she helped him to his feet. After they all were up she told them, "I will need one final blood sample from each of you." The men groaned in unison. They were tired of all this poking and prodding.

Once the blood was taken she told them that would be all for the day, and they should take this opportunity to explore the culture the city had to offer, and not so much of its wine. With controlled excitement, she brought the samples of blood to Oman in his laboratory. On a wall he projected the magnified view of the new samples, and compared them to the blood taken from the group the first day. Scrutinizing the images he pointed to a grayish-white cell that looked like a fuzzy ball of hair in the image of the blood samples just taken. From his mind he communicated, *This is it, the new Tau cell complex. The serum works. You can tell them they no longer need fear that disease. I shall inform Atar.*

Rhonda was so relieved. She was very proud of Oman and her people. The free sharing of their knowledge with all should show the planet the meaning of cooperation. She departed the laboratory in search of the group of men. She was so excited; she wanted to tell them the results as soon as possible.

Atar sent for the secretary—said to meet him outside the island's hydroponics farm. Upon his arrival Atar greeted him and said, "I know you have been busy with the council setting up a treaty, but you really have not opened up with us and told us your country's needs. You also have not taken much time to explore our city. The only thing you have really shown an interest in is obtaining the cure to that disease you called AIDS."

Taking him by the shoulder, Atar guided him into the hydroponics farm. "Have you not wondered how we have survived all these millennia at the bottom of, what you call, the Atlantic Ocean? Look about you. This is where part of that miracle is created. From this small building we feed our people. We have devised our own gas mixture for breathing."

Arthur was taking this all in. He compared, in his mind, their isolation at the bottom of the ocean to the isolation of space. Atar continued, "From talks we have had with the others we discovered that your kind wish to explore space, and that for a period of time both your country and that of the country you call Russia had some sort of contest or race to propel yourselves into space. From what I have learned, this was a time when your technology increased exponentially, and your emphasis on developing weapons of annihilation took a secondary position. I believe that this is a better task upon which to direct your energies."

He stared hard at the secretary to see his reaction to the next question, Atar paused then continued, "What would you say if I could give the means to return to that *space race*? I can provide your people with the wherewithal to live and to colonize in space."

The secretary was stunned. His mind reeled with the possibilities, but he could not get himself to answer. Atar just said, "Think about it, and remember what I have said and shown you. Discuss it with your government. Peace can be obtained, and so can the conquest of space." Taking a goblet from a tray he had a servant prepare, Atar gave the secretary something to drink. "Here," Atar handed him the goblet, "take this and drink. It will make you feel better."

The secretary graciously accepted, "Thank you," and drank the sweet-tasting drink. It was refreshing, but it gave him an odd sensation—all those distinctively different flavors in one glass. "Very refreshing, thank you. What was it?" the secretary asked. A moment later he collapsed to the floor. In exactly ten minutes he began to stir into wakefulness again.

"Wha—what happened?" inquired the secretary, as he climbed to his feet.

Atar smiled amusedly, and answered, "It appears we get the same reaction to the serum from everyone who imbibes it." Pausing a moment to let that statement sink into the diplomat's mind, Atar then concluded, "You no longer need worry about that disease ever again."

Shocked, the secretary asked, "You mean the serum works?"

"Is that not what I just said?" remarked Atar whimsically.

Very much excited the secretary asked, "I don't have to worry about AIDS the rest of my life?" Atar just nodded affirmation. "Wow!" the secretary exclaimed, losing all sense of decorum. "I've got to report this to the president, right away!" he shouted and ran off to find Raval, and have him transport him to the ship so he could make his report.

In Washington the news was received with as much excitement. The president was so overwhelmed with happiness; he was almost in tears when he called for a press conference.

When the news of the Atlantian achievement spread around the world, the celebration which followed surpassed that done at the end of the second millennia; which ushered in the 21st century. This global party lasted a full two weeks before showing any sign of diminishing, and for those all too few days the world was truly at peace.

CHAPTER THIRTEEN

In the weeks that followed the president's address to the nation declaring that the cure to AIDS had been found, and it was discovered by the once lost civilization of Atlantis, the world seemed to clamor at the door of Atlantis. Scientists and statesmen alike begged an audience with the council of ten. Much curiosity and speculation was made about them by the media. Finally, after considerable deliberation, the council consented to a worldwide television broadcast to dispel the skepticism, and to announce their existence as a new nation.

Arthur Franks had returned to their island a week earlier to conclude the formalizing of the United States treaty and trade agreements with Atlantis. The Russians had sent their diplomats as well, as did the countries of the European Union.

Finally, after they had signed the treaties that identified them as a new sovereign nation of the world, the Atlantians opened their harbor once more to do trade with the other nations of the world. The only limitations the Atlantians imposed on their new visitors were the number of citizens each ship could allow to embark upon their island. The Atlantians, as a whole, took most of this in stride, but being a new nation brought about new problems. For a country which used the barter system of trade, now to have to use currency, and to accept other nations as well was disconcerting.

Atar had arranged for communication equipment to be installed near the harbor to aid in controlling the ever-increasing flow of traffic and trade. Now Atlantis could communicate with the rest of the world.

The council did manage an exchange of earth's technologies for Atlantian bioscience. Atlantis was teeming with life, most of which were scientists from around the world. This was the place to be. The new frontier on the biosciences was being explored here. Atlantis even sent out some of their young specialists to many of the world's famous colleges and universities to establish proficiency in their newly acquired technology. The emphasis was an exchange of knowledge, but in doing so the council demanded that no one was to disclose the existence of Atlantian telepathy, Aquarians, or Ular. Nor was anyone to demonstrate any feats of strength greater than that of a typical surface dweller. The Atlantians began to blend in with the rest of humanity, and all the time gaining more knowledge.

On the day that marked one month from their rising, Sara came into the life science building to talk over a personal matter with Rhonda. "I think that I am with child," Sara remarked bluntly to her friend. "My cycle has not come, and I have never been late before."

Looking at her friend with consoling eyes, Rhonda asked, "How could that be? You haven't known any man who has not been under control—have you?"

Flushed, Sara replied, "I was with that surface dweller at the time of his capture, but…" she said with confusion, "I thought all men were under control."

"Apparently not," Rhonda noted as she started her examination. "If you are with child do you want to carry it full term?" Sara thought for a moment. She hadn't considered fully the possibility of having a child. She was uncertain. Before she could formulate an answer Rhonda said, "I wonder which side of the union will dominate?"

"What do you mean?" inquired Sara.

"Oh, come on—think. You said that he was a surface dweller. I'm sure you've noticed some of the differences. I've been studying their bios and found that their life string embodies one more chromatin than we have, yet they have not developed any of their potentials. Setting all that aside, we are stronger, quicker, and more intelligent. On one test I gave the surface dwellers they barely did better than a Soschatch, and you know how subhuman they are."

"Oh!" Sara gasped. "I didn't think that such a union could produce anything less than that of our own." Sara began to weep.

"There, there," Rhonda said comfortingly while patting Sara's back. "I was just speculating on the negative side, so you might be better prepared to make your decision. We have no hard facts in this direction. Yours would be the first union since the holocaust. And there is that extra *chromatin* I mentioned. We don't know what it will do—yet," Rhonda said trying to lift her friend's spirits.

"I understand," Sara replied, wiping the tears from her eyes. "I just hope you are wrong." Pausing, she then asked Rhonda, "Will Oman have to be told?"

"I think he should, considering that extra chromatin; but no one else need know," Rhonda simply stated.

"Oh well, I guess you're right," Sara said with resignation.

"Here, drink this," instructed Rhonda as she gave Sara a glass of light green liquid. "This is a refinement of all the antigens both natural and produced found in our systems and that of the surface dwellers. It will give your baby the head start it needs." In moments Sara swooned to the floor, and then started to stir minutes later. "Of course, I still haven't found a way around that side effect," Rhonda said with a laugh.

Oman strolled in as Rhonda was laughing, and thought to Rhonda, *Why the laughter?*

Rhonda related to Oman the events of the past few minutes, and that the side effect was still a bit amusing to her. Oman agreed and pondered, *What's this I picked up about Sara being with child?*

Oman instructed Rhonda, *Have your friend return here once a cycle for a checkup and we shall chart the baby's progress. We shall see what we can do to help her along and ensure that the baby has all the benefits we can bestow upon him.*

Him? Rhonda shot an inquiring thought to Oman.

Why yes, came a chuckling thought from Oman. *From reading your minds I have discovered that the man who impregnated our Sara is the same man named John whose blood and body fluids we have been testing.*

So, replied Rhonda.

So, you are not as observant as I believed I taught you to be. John's seed is decidedly slanted toward the male gender. Now do you see? Oman chuckled into her mind.

Rhonda didn't bother to reply. He knew his answer. She turned to her friend, Sara, and gave her the good news. Sara was delighted.

Work progressed in many of the space laboratories around the world. Governments were increasing their budgets to further the exploration of space, and now with the promise of Atlantian help, the race was on once more. Every country involved in space exploration was seeking the assistance of an Atlantian specialist.

During the next eight months Atlantis had established itself as the leader in the biosciences. With their help, new spaceship designs were being developed, new alloys created, even better forms of propulsion were being gleaned by the scientists. The United States joined with the European Space Agency and Japan on a joint venture to produce the world's largest orbital habitat. It was designed to house two thousand people, and in it they could build a factory for the future production and launching of manned space probes. The entire construction would be self-sustaining. People could live there all their life long. It was even conceived to have a school, and later a university. Big plans indeed, but now with the Atlantian's push to the stars it seemed like anything was possible. The only drawback in the scheme of things was the twelve-year completion date. Many of the new substances used in this great undertaking had to be manufactured in space in its zero gravity. This was to be done, assured the Atlantian scientists, to create a life station that would not deteriorate with time.

Sara had made her cyclic visits to the life science building without fail. Rhonda and Oman watched over her with great interest. When asked, Oman told her that he himself was not sure if the baby would be like that of an Atlantian or of a surface dweller. He could only promise the baby a long and healthy life. He had introduced into the fetus the enzymes necessary to bestow all the gifts he had created or could control. With the approval of the council of ten the baby was given telepathy, strength, endurance, speed, and the Aquarian traits of his mother, and yet, with all these, Oman did not know what that extra chromatin would cause. He surmised that it would either cancel out all his hard work or perhaps effectively enhance each trait.

Now was the time to find out. Sara had come full term, and soon the baby would be born. With gentle hands, Rhonda aided Sara in giving birth to her son. He was beautiful and perfect. The first thing Rhonda noticed was his gills. On the center of his chest were three folds of skin. Rhonda gently took a swab and cleared the mucus from them with a saline solution. As she did so he opened his big wide eyes and started to breath. She then gave Sara her newborn son, all pink and soft. "Have you chosen a name for him yet?" asked Rhonda with a smile.

"Yes, I have. I shall name him Serik after my grandfather."

"Serik is a wonderful name," cooed Rhonda.

Oman just observed the blessed event. His calculating mind understood that a union with the surface dwellers was not only possible, but possibly beneficial. He noted the gills with glee. At least he was one of them. He wondered what his destiny would be. He had been given every gift Oman knew of. He was Atlantian! Oman turned and walked away to let the two girls talk woman talk.

The United Nations sent emissaries to Atlantis to formally invite them to join their organization. When the council of ten assembled to meet with these emissaries and hear their offer, Atar was the one to address them. "I regret that you have come all this way for nothing. It has been, and always shall be, the policy of our nation never to get involved with the petty political squabbles of this plant. We do not condone nor dissuade. We wish only to remain neutral, to trade freely with all nations, and to aid and assist all peoples if we can. The very nature of your political processes is barbaric to us, inasmuch as how you treat one another as nations, and therefore we decline your gracious offer."

The emissaries were dumbfounded. This offer was not made lightly, nor to all nations of the world. In fact, Atlantis was the only nation ever to refuse to join the UN since its founding in 1945. Before they could voice a protest, or formulate reasons why Atlantis should reconsider and join the UN, Tempest spoke up, "We thank you for your time, but we have more pressing business to discuss. Raval shall escort you back to the harbor and your vessel. Perhaps in time your peoples will understand."

Raval then stepped up to the two and escorted them out of the citadel.

Tempest turned to Atar and asked, "Do you think it wise to continually snub the surface dweller's attempts at making us fit in? The world has changed since Atlantis was the center of government and most powerful nation."

"I understand your concern, my dear friend, but we must keep ourselves separate from any political allegiance, so as to better guide mankind. Already we have diverted their energies, once directed toward the making of weapons, into further exploration of space. The council has deployed search teams to try to locate the lost knowledge our ancestors sent to the four corners of the world. Believe me, this is the better way."

"I suppose you are correct. Your wisdom has not failed us yet."

From birth, Oman knew that Serik would grow up to be a very special child. Oman often contemplated that when the time came he would personally instruct Serik in the biosciences. This lad would be his protégé, and someday his successor.

A year had passed since Serik was born. It was time for his first annual checkup. A blood sample was taken, and the usual degrees showed more freedom of motion in the axis of his shoulders, and yet no indications of a malformed ball and socket joint. On one test she had him hold his breath. When he did so she found that he could hold it as long as she could. This sparked more interest in his development, and so Rhonda continued other tests of coordination and dexterity. Each test demonstrated superior abilities to those recorded for children his age.

Oman stepped into the examination room and instantly realized what Rhonda had discovered. He then went to his office and returned with a small projection device and a stack of various colored gelatin slides. He set the device up on the table nearest Serik, and demonstrated how the unit was operated. Showing Serik a red gel and projecting that light on the wall he thought to Serik, *Do you know what color that is?* Serik nodded affirmatively.

What is it?

Serik replied, "Red!"

Pulling out the red gel Oman replaced it with a green one. *And this color?* Oman thought to Serik continuing his line of questioning.

Serik answered, "Green!" and smiled, enjoying all this attention.

Oman then replaced the green gel with a blue one, and thought, *This one?*

Serik thought a moment then answered, "Blue!"

Excellent! thought Oman. *Now watch what happens when I put all three colors together.* He projected the new hue. Serik was captivated with awe. *What color do they make together?* thought Oman once more to Serik.

"Ahh—white!" Serik spoke out in a burst.

That is correct! thought Oman. *See the many colors you can make from the different slides. Here, you go on and take this projector home with you. Have fun, and see if you can remember all the primary colors and their various combinations.* Oman turned to Rhonda to have her explain to Sara that he had given Serik the projector. *It will help him learn his colors, and prepare him for his future studies on light wavelengths, and the maser's different functions.*

Rhonda just gave a knowing smile. She really didn't believe he gave Serik the device purely as a training aid. She remembered having something similar as a toy while she was growing up.

As the years passed Serik grew in stature and developed into a very bright and inquisitive youth. On his seventh yearly checkup he demonstrated an ability for long range telepathy. He was introduced to Ular, and quickly made friends with the gigantic living brain. Through Serik, Ular was able to sense more of his fellow Atlantian's world and now the whole earth.

At this same time work was progressing well on the space station. It was over fifty percent completed. Portions of the living quarters and breathable mixtures plant were finished which allowed the workmen a place to live. Artificial gravity hadn't been installed, as the rotating station hampered work in certain areas. That portion wouldn't be installed until the outer shell was complete. Sending materials up to the station was slow and very costly. A small work force had established a base on the moon to extract minerals there. On the moon a small dome shaped structure provided the only protection for the work camp. Constant monitoring of the structure's outer skin had to be done as the continuous bombardment of cosmic dust was eroding it away. These continuous repairs to the skin hindered the work crew's ability to produce ore at full capacity.

On earth, Atar had sent his daughter and other parties in search of the old knowledge. On one expedition a group discovered an ancient, lost Nahuatl temple in Guatemala; and another later expedition, that Atar's daughter led, discovered a sealed vault within a pyramid-shaped building discovered deep in the mountains of Peru. Inside were carvings and statues similar to ancient Atlantian design and a coffer. The coffer was returned to Atlantis and opened there. Inside they found a scroll of papyrus written in the old cuneiform inscription. This was part of the old knowledge, most of which, they later learned, were of things they had known of or recently discovered. There was also a reference to more stored knowledge encased in a large figure of a sphinx in the land of the morning sun. More exploration was necessary before they exhausted every possible location of Atlantian influence.

Another six years of unproductive searching went by until the Atlantian's meticulous inspection of the Sphinx in Egypt revealed a hidden, sealed room. The walls to this room were nine feet thick. The Egyptian authorities were reluctant to allow the Atlantians permission to open the sealed room, until Tempest arrived on the scene. Somehow Tempest was able to convince the Department Head of Egyptian Antiquities that not only should the Atlantian expedition be allowed to open the room, but also that it was the Atlantian's right to do so.

Once the room was opened a virtual storehouse of information was revealed. It was as if they had opened the Atlantian version of the Library of Congress. Formulas and notes of experiments on genetic research and alterations were revealed. Much of the lost knowledge was now restored.

At this same time, Serik reached thirteen years of age on the Gregorian calendar. He had developed total recall from his memory training, and he now was able to communicate with Ular at even greater distances. No positive link-up was necessary. He was the first one to be able to do that. Besides his ability to read thoughts, he was learning to inject them. He was maturing very fast, and understood completely the responsibility of his gifts. Oman made sure of this. He was starting his studies with Oman on the biosciences, and now the old knowledge of genetic engineering. He had just completed his training with the maser, and soon he would be sent to the outside, as it was now called, to be taught the technical sciences. This was to include robotics, telecommunications, computers, digital electronics, and laser research. He was fluent in English, Russian, French, Spanish, as well as his own native tongue. After he learned Arabic, Japanese, and Chinese he hoped to learn Navaho. What he heard about the American Indians and the ancient ones of Central and South America intrigued him.

On this annual examination, Oman took him into the examination room alone. *I have been charting the progress of your development, Serik. I have noticed your ease of learning, your physical stamina, and your mental prowess. All of these are exceptional*, Oman thought to Serik.

Why, thank you, Oman, Serik thought back to him, accepting his compliment.

Oman continued, *That is not all. Your biochemistry is changing, and my tests have concluded it is due to that extra chromatin you inherited from your father. Not only that, but from what I have observed you are entering your next phase of development, called puberty. If my calculations are correct this stage of development will cause even more drastic changes in your inherent abilities. One of these new traits, I am expecting you to develop, is the ability to levitate objects.*

How can I do that? questioned Serik's thoughts.

Oman placed a metallic rod on the table in front of Serik, then answered. *I believe that this may be done similarly to blowing a feather. In your mind you take a deep breath, relax a moment, and then blow in one direction. Not having the ability or knowing of anyone who can makes it difficult for me to teach you, but I think by picturing in your mind the action you wish to accomplish and projecting that thought, like blowing the feather, can cause it to happen. Here, try moving this rod.*

As Oman gestured to the metallic rod, Serik thought in his mind as if the rod was a feather and to blow it to cause it to move. His attempt failed. Oman encouraged him to try again. Serik did so, and again the same results. The metallic rod didn't budge. Oman sensed Serik's despondency, and suggested. *Relax. Relax. Take a moment to breathe and believe you can do it because believing in yourself is the key. Relax.*

Serik took a deep breath then exhaled slowly. He let his mind empty and then he filled it with the thought of blowing a feather. In his mind he took a deep breath and, still relaxed, he focused his attention on the metallic rod and blew. Still the rod remained unyielding.

Perhaps not enough of a change has occurred in your body, or perhaps I am wrong altogether. It really isn't that important. Don't worry about it, Oman thought consolingly.

Serik wouldn't allow himself to believe his mentor could ever be wrong about anything. His emotions started to rise, and in his mind he took a deep breath, relaxed slightly, focused his attention on the metallic rod, and blew hard believing he could move it, and that such an act was easy, second nature. As he did so the rod twitched then spun around slowly. Serik had moved the rod. He showed that this latent talent was his to control.

Very good—Serik! came Oman's thought of congratulations.

During the next few months of intensive training Serik began to learn the secrets of bioengineering. One day he turned to Oman and projected a questioning thought, *Whatever happened to the earlier creations—such as the centaur, satyr, griffin, and the like? I mean—if they existed once why don't they exist now?*

Oman stopped what he was doing, and reminisced, *We didn't really* know what to expect back then when these first kinds of experiments began, so as a safeguard each creature was made asexual so it could not reproduce if the experiment was unfavorable.

With a thoughtful nod, Serik replied, "I see." Then he decided to query another thought. *Has this always been serious work, or has any of this research been for fun?*

Oman anticipated this question and answered, *The marfle was made for the enjoyment of the children, as a pet, but I don't think that is what you meant when you asked the question. Well, if you promise to keep it a secret I'll tell you. A long time ago, the earliest group of bioengineers was getting bored with their work, and one of the younger engineers of the group suggested that they make something really strange, and so they did. Remember some of your lessons on the animals living today around the world? The one called the duck-billed platypus is the result of that experiment.*

"Wow!" was Serik's only reply.

As if nothing had happened the two went back to work.

CHAPTER FOURTEEN

The *New Hope* space station was now fully operational. Not only were the solar cells producing enough energy to sustain it, but the excess was being beamed down to earth in a split waveform to each nation that was part of this project. The space station was in geosynchronous orbit over north central Canada to best transmit this energy to each country.

Scheduled super-shuttle flights to the station were becoming commonplace. New concepts in interstellar engines were being tested, and as such experiments were being carried out, an approved design in a spacecraft was being built with metals similar to that which made up the space station. Tenth-generation computer systems were being installed; each circuit being covered with a thin layer of sapphire to enhance its durability.

Back on earth nuclear disarmament was taking place. It was hoped that the next generation would be able to grow up in a world of peace.

Another six years had passed. The world was finally at peace; turning from nuclear power to geothermal, with the aid of the Atlantians, had helped to bring this about. Automobiles were being driven on the plasma energy of hydrogen gas. No longer did the weather report in Los Angeles give a pollution index. The air was becoming cleaner. The coal industry did not suffer in the change of energy. In fact, they were the first industry to convert to the new power.

Serik had finished his education on Atlantis and from the *outside* as well. He had brought the biosciences to the stars. The center of the space station remained a weightless void to aid in experiments that required zero gravity. Serik had transferred to the *New Hope,* and was able to develop a strain of bacteria that could only first exist in weightless space. Later he mutated it to a strain that could survive gravity. This he then turned into a serum to cure leukemia. He was becoming well known around the world. Some called him the Pasteur of the 21st century.

On his occasional visits back home he would often go for a swim with Raval. Their dives to the ocean's bottom were now becoming commonplace. After all, being an Aquarian did have some benefits. On these occasions Serik would collect plants from the bottom, and would use them in various attempts to finding the ultimate vaccine. One day he would, he promised himself.

Oman was doing an experiment with Ular. He was trying to attempt cellular division of a central lobe, and retaining a portion of his conscience, a sort of genetic memory. Ular projected that he wanted to go among the stars. He was taught all there was to know about the stars, the universe, celestial navigation, and three dimensional geometry. Oman's experiment turned out to be a success. Not exactly a clone, but instead a miniature of Ular was created, a sort of twin. In unison each segment conveyed the same thought, *I am alive!* Oman worked for the next two months to contrive a portable living station for Ular's new twin. Immersed in a special embryonic fluid, Ular II was encased in a uniquely constructed geodesic sphere.

While Oman was busy assembling this sphere some of the Atlantian soothsayers had met in counsel with the council of ten to discuss, what they believed to be, the forthcoming end of the world.

"Look for yourself," one of the soothsayers said. "There have been an ever-increasing number of earthquakes reported around the world. Last week parts of Southern California were devastated when the

San Andreas Fault shifted. The result was an earthquake with a force equivalent to eight on the Richter scale, as measured by the surface dwellers. This is the third such recorded earthquake of this magnitude in just the past week alone. We have concluded that this is just the prelude to what will come next. From what we can discern, that fault is like the keystone to the world. When it finally shifts loose, the world as we know it will be no more. The earth shall either crumble into an asteroid belt, or turn nova and change to a star. The end result is the same. The earth is about to be destroyed, and there is no way to relieve the pressure anywhere else on earth."

"You are certain of your findings?" Atar inquired.

"As certain as anyone can be on this matter," the soothsayer reluctantly assured him.

Atar and the rest of the council were dismayed. Now what were they to do? There was no sense informing the other leaders of the world. They probably wouldn't believe them anyway.

"Any idea as to how long before this event occurs?" asked Atar.

The eldest soothsayer replied, "We predict sometime in the next six lunar cycles. Precisely when is hard to tell, but we have at least one lunar cycle to prepare."

Atar contemplated—one lunar cycle. Not much time to construct a spaceship. Then a thought struck him. He turned to one of the council's attendants and telepathically instructed him to seek out Serik and have him come before the council.

The attendant returned a slight bow of acknowledgment and stated, "By your leave," then turned and departed the chamber.

Returning his attention to the soothsayers, Atar emphasized, "I trust you will remain silent of this. It would serve no one to tell the others. We do not need a panic."

"We have never questioned your wisdom, sire, nor shall we now."

With an affirmative gesture Atar dismissed the soothsayers. He then turned his attention to the council and projected, *Join with me.*

Each member of the council relaxed, eyes closed and minds opened, joined with Atar's thoughts. In this quiet moment Atar explained his plan.

Serik had been visiting with his mother, who was still as beautiful as before he was born, when the council's messenger arrived. "Your presence is required of the council," the servant flatly stated to Serik.

"I understand. I shall proceed shortly." The servant took this as an affirmative to Atar's command and departed. Serik turned to face his mother. "I must go. It must be urgent or the council wouldn't have sent for me." Leaning over to her, he gave her a kiss and spoke, "I love you. Thank you for my life." He gathered what few things he had brought with him and departed.

Sara stayed in the doorway to watch him go until he was out of sight. A tear swelled on her cheek as she silently mouthed the words, "I love you, too." She was extremely proud of him. He was the most accomplished Atlantian in known history. He excelled at whatever task he chose to endeavor.

Once inside the citadel, Serik made straight for the council chamber. As the great doors swung open to usher him in, he could sense the tension in the air. With a respectful bow he projected, *My lords*, and patiently awaited their reply.

Tempest's thoughts were the first to touch his mind. *We have received some grievous news. What information we are about to share with you must not leave this room. Is that understood?*

Yes, I understand.

Mord then inquired, *Are you still working at the space station?*

Yes.

Mord continued his questions. *Has the space ark been completed yet?*

No, not yet. It is scheduled for completion in three weeks, as the world measures time, and anticipating the next question, he continued, *The following week will be utilized for system check-outs, and the week after for a test flight.*

Atar posed the next question. *Do you feel that a test flight is actually necessary, or do you think the ship could handle an extended flight straight away?*

Considering this question for a moment, he responded, *I have noted their work in progress on the ship, and know that many Atlantians have helped in its construction. With that in mind, I feel that the craft is more than ready.*

Atar was pleased with this answer, and continued, *Before we reveal to you what it is that distresses us so, I have two more questions. How many persons is this ship designed to sustain on an indefinitely long space probe? And, is there a way to transport one of our submersibles to the space station and place it within a storeroom on the craft?*

Serik was quick to reply. *It was designed to house twenty passengers. As to the submersible, it would have to be brought up in a supply run, and marked as instruments or apparatus. Once it is there I can arrange to have it taken on board the space ark, but may I ask now, why all these questions?*

Atar, in agreement with the council, responded, *You may. It has to do with the information we were given earlier this day. I am sure you were told of the events leading to our island being hurtled to the surface. An accident occurred when we tried to relieve the pressure on a fault. This was done to save our city. The soothsayer's predictions have more than once aided our home. Now, these same men have told us that soon the whole planet will be split wide open, and either crumble to dust or explode, going nova and transforming this planet into a star.*

Shouldn't we warn the rest of the world? asked Serik in astonishment.

Atar answered him with a question. *Would you want to start a world-wide panic? How many could get off this planet? It would be futile. The earth, with all its technology, could not construct enough spaceships in time. In fact, the space ark is the only vehicle able to do what must be done.*

What is that? inquired Serik.

To preserve what we can of our culture, and to colonize another planet so that the human race is not made extinct, answered Atar.

Then who is going to play God and choose which individuals will be allowed to live? Serik retorted.

Resignedly, Atar answered, *We, of the council, have made that decision. You represent our greatest success in genetic engineering. Being the culmination of Atlantian and surface dweller, you are the most skilled and knowledgeable person on this planet. Oman has successfully cloned Ular who can act as your navigator and mass storage of all acquired knowledge.*

Who will be the others?

Ravel, Rhonda, and my daughter, Hellena, will accompany you. Our best estimate is that a total of three men and three women have the best chance for survival. We also wish to include two surface dwellers; one male and one female. If you have any friends that seem healthy enough we want you to enlist them in this quest, so the final decision who will accompany you will be yours.

Just great! Now you want me to play God, retorted Serik in disgust.

If it is of any help, you will need a computer programmer/technician, and a propulsion engineer to bring along with you. We hope that some of your friends will match your needs. If so, the decision is made for you, and you will not have to feel as if you are playing God, as you put it. Pausing a moment, Atar continued with an anger he seldom displayed. *Can you not understand—this is survival! You and the people we have chosen will be all that remains of mankind. We have calculated your best chance of survival, and the people best suited for this task and for repopulating a planet. I love life and would go if I could, but that is not the case. I am not qualified. I—we all envy you. Do not throw your gifts away. Use them as they were intended, to better mankind! If mankind is no more then why even try? We are giving you a chance to help the human race survive. Your duty is to accept. Look at the trust we are bestowing upon you. Do not fail us. You know as well as I that with great ability comes great responsibility!* Atar sat down, exhausted both physically and mentally.

Serik, now humbled, agreed with the council. Turning to face Atar, he felt an inner pride for his people growing within his being. He bowed deeply with respect before departing the citadel, resolved to the task assigned to him. He knew what must be done.

"Send for Oman," commanded Atar. "There is much he must prepare for."

One of the attendants went to fetch Oman. Sensing the seriousness that caused him to be sent for, the instant he arrived Oman projected to the council, *You have a need?*

A grievous need, replied Atar. *As expedient as possible we require of you to have Ular II absorb the recovered knowledge. We also need you to ensure his ability to navigate in space, and to have him ready for an extended trip.*

Why the urgency?

My friend, Atar started, *the time has finally come when the world shall end.*

Oman was momentarily stunned. *When?*

Soon, sometime within the next six lunar cycles, Atar flatly answered.

Will any survive?

We have discussed a way in which Rhonda, Serik, Hellena, and Raval, along with two surface dwellers shall steal away in the space ark, and hopefully be able to repopulate another world. Ular II will be needed as navigator and be their knowledge holder. Can you prepare him soon? He must be ready to depart in two weeks' time, then to be shipped up to the space station. We cannot warn the world, even with their advanced technology there just is not enough time. If we told them it would only cause a worldwide panic.

It shall be done, Oman projected to the council, turned, and returned to his lab.

Serik worked with Raval to crate one of the more powerful submersibles. With the aid of a few Soschatch, and a large block and tackle, they commenced to hoist the submersible out of the harbor. Once it was raised sufficiently, Raval helped to guide it onto a waiting pallet. Just as the group had it centered over the platform, the cable parted. The heavy submersible came careening down. Suddenly, as if a giant invisible hand had reached out and grabbed it, the submersible's descent stopped. It hovered over Raval, who had ducked when it started to fall toward him. Raval took this opportunity to scramble to safety as beads of sweat formed on Serik's forehead. With a long sigh of relief, Serik gently levitated the huge craft onto the pallet, setting it there to rest.

Raval was amazed at what he'd just witnessed. He stared at Serik and uttered, "I didn't know you could do that!"

Serik looked back at him with a bewildered expression and responded, "I didn't know I could either."

After regaining their composure, Raval and Serik were able to finish crating the huge submersible. "Why do you think the council wants us to take the submersible along?" Serik inquired.

"I really don't know unless they suspect that the planet we'll be going to is covered with water, or perhaps, in their wisdom, they want us to be prepared for anything."

"Well, I had better go and make arrangements for my new apparatus to be shipped up to the space station. Can you take me to Florida?" inquired Serik.

"I can have you there by midmorning," Raval claimed as he escorted Serik into his waiting craft.

Getting the clearances for his apparatus was harder than he had anticipated. At first the project manager balked, but how could he refuse the award-winning Serik. Serik had won the Nobel Prize for his research and development of the serum that cured leukemia.

"New experiment?" the project manager asked in his New England accent.

"Yes," answered Serik. "Cure to cancer," he said matter-of-factly.

"The experiment is time critical. I'll need this device sent up in the next shuttle," Serik emphasized.

"Wow, that is important," remarked the project manager lifting an eyebrow. "OK then, what are its dimensions and weight?"

The project manager was stunned by Serik's description. "I'll have to get clearance from NASA on that big of a payload. Do you have room for it in your work center? Never mind, wait here and I'll call NASA." The project manager departed, and went to the phone in his office. Ten minutes later he emerged from his office. Puzzled, he walked over to Serik, "I don't know who you know, but it must be someone important. I've been instructed to make room for your apparatus even if it means holding back the new solar mirror." Pausing to regain his composure, he then asked, "Where is it?"

"I'll have it here two days prior to liftoff. Now if you will excuse me, I have some more errands to run before the day is over." He departed, leaving behind a very confused project manager.

CHAPTER FIFTEEN

A tar, Tempest, and Mord did their part to help things along. For the second time since the island surfaced, the three representatives of the Atlantian nation departed their island home.

They went to the headquarters of WASP [World Avionics and Space Program] located in London, England. This was where all the planning and project scheduling for the space station took place. This was also where the schedule for tests of the space ark *Andromeda* were decided. As the three men approached the executive secretary, they learned the protocol that would open the necessary doors. "Tell Mr. O'Gill that the leaders of Atlantis have arrived and wish to speak with him on a matter of great importance to all mankind. You may say that Atar is here. Now hurry, my time is precious." Atar spoke confidently as he looked down upon the secretary. No secret hid from his probing eyes.

The secretary nervously switched the intercom on and made her announcement, "Mr. O'Gill, a Mr. Atar is here. He claims that he is the leader of Atlantis, and wishes to speak with you of a matter, he claims, important to all mankind."

Before the secretary could switch off her intercom, Mr. O'Gill rushed to his door, opened it up to Atar and his companions, and graciously ushered them in. "Welcome, Mr. Atar. Please come in. This is quite an honor for me. What may I do to help you?" Before Atar could answer him, Mr. O'Gill turned to his secretary and instructed, "Hold all my calls, and don't disturb us," as he closed the door behind them.

Turning around to face the trio, Mr. O'Gill asked, "Can I offer any of you something to drink?"

"No, that will not be necessary," replied Atar for the trio. "Our time is very precious. There is much we must do."

"Oh—I see," remarked Mr. O'Gill. "What is so important that you came all this way to see me?"

"We understand that all the projects, tests, and such goings on of the space station are scheduled here. Is that correct?" inquired Atar.

"Why, yes. That is correct," he replied. Feeling a bit ill at ease with the three men standing, he added, "Won't you please have a seat?"

"No, thank you, Mr. O'Gill. We will only take a few more moments of your time. Just a few questions more, but please take your own seat and relax," stated Atar.

There was something about the suggestion to sit down that compelled Mr. O'Gill to do so. *Relax*, came the next thought that entered his mind.

Who has the final say as to the scheduled events at the space station, and what must be done to change them?

Mr. O'Gill felt a bit odd. He heard the question, or thought he heard the question, but Atar's lips weren't moving. Pausing a moment to collect his thoughts, he answered, "I have the final say. It is my signature that approves the schedule. To change it I need only send a memo to the project manager. He in turn arranges the necessary tasks to be done."

"Thank you, Mr. O'Gill. You have been most helpful. We have one small change we would like you to make to your scheduled test flight of the space ark," Atar continued as the other two Atlantians positioned themselves on either side of Mr. O'Gill. "We feel that it would make a better test if you were to arrange to have the space ark totally outfitted to capacity with fuel, food and provisions, spare parts, breathing mixtures—everything. That way the entire testing would be compressed to one flight, and every aspect checked out thoroughly."

"Yes, you are right. I'll do that now," agreed Mr. O'Gill. He took his pen and wrote out the necessary memo.

Thank you, came a soothing voice from within. "When we go you shall only remember that this was your own idea, and you will see to it that it gets done. As for our visit...." Atar stopped and Tempest took over.

"As for our visit—we shall leave with you the information necessary to build and install a filter that will broaden the bandwidth of your microwave transmitter, and change the frequency output. By doing so it will induce a magnetic field set at the precise frequency needed to kill all insects that transmit disease. We have recently learned that these disease infested insects can be destroyed this way by sympathetic harmonics, and yet not harm the other productive insects or mankind. In one quick swoop many epidemics will cease to exist. Mord has written down the design and specifications, time durations and such. If you adhere to them strictly your task will be successful. Consider it another gift from your neighbors, the Atlantians."

Mr. O'Gill came out of his daze just as Atar extended his hand in friendship. "We thank you for your time. We know how busy you must be. We hope our suggestion will be of some help," Atar concluded.

"Thank you for your time, and I will send your ideas down to development," Mr. O'Gill said cheerfully, and escorted the trio from his office. As he did so he called to his secretary. "Miss Grant, I have a memo I want sent to the project manager immediately, and after you get done with that, come in, I have a cover letter to dictate on this new filter the Atlantians designed for us." He handed her the memo he had written under the Atlantian influence, and then returned to his office.

A week later Serik returned to Atlantis. Oman had just concluded aiding Ular II in the absorption process of the recovered knowledge as well as his course on celestial navigation. Serik was swimming near the ocean's bottom, he figured for the last time. Serik's mother was there to greet him at the harbor. When he emerged from the submersible she caught a glimpse of him and her eyes started to water. When he walked up to her she was on the verge of crying. He looked down on her and she hugged him and said, "The council told me of your mission. I will miss you very much."

"I will miss you too, but as long as I have memory you shall never be forgotten," he assured her.

Rhonda now came to join them, "The council and I decided not to waste space, so we enclosed in the submersible a wealth of seeds and chemicals to help us on our journey. I've included some special test equipment and medical supplies. That, along with what I understand will be placed on board the space ark, should be more than sufficient."

"Why are you so cheerful? Don't you realize that our home, our planet will soon be destroyed? All our loved ones will perish!" Serik condemningly directed to Rhonda.

Rhonda's smile left her face. She gathered her resolve and said, "Look here! You have no right to talk to me that way! Sure I care, but crying over things I cannot change won't help a thing. Life is hard at best. It continually throws obstacles in our way. These obstacles then become opportunities to better ourselves. Why the council chose *you* to lead this group is beyond me, if that is your attitude. It would better suit you and our mission if you thought about this as an adventure."

Serik was taken aback. Rhonda was correct. He was just feeling sorry for himself about being separated permanently from his mother. "I am sorry," Serik replied. "You are right. Will you forgive me?"

Rhonda's cheery smile returned and she answered, "Sure."

During the next two days, arrangements were made to ship the crate marked *apparatus*. Ular II would be taken with the group when they departed. The Atlantians had chartered a modified Royal Air Force Chinook HC MKI helicopter from a commercial shipper in Bermuda. The pilot flew to *Skyoil-One*, refueled, and hovered over the island. At a prearranged location he landed. There eight Soschatch, Raval, and Serik helped to load the huge crate. Once onboard Raval paid the pilot in gold and said to everyone, "I'm going to accompany the crate. My first mate, Kile, will take the rest of you to Florida. I shall meet you at Cape Kennedy."

With a nod of understanding, the others backed away as the pilot revved up the engines. After they were airborne he informed Raval, "Just so you know, we will have to stop at the derrick to top off our fuel and again in Bermuda. Our ETA for Cape Kennedy is about twelve hours."

After saying their goodbyes, and a few hugs and tears later, Serik, Rhonda, and Hellena were on their way to Florida. Serik had made arrangements for a limousine to meet them at the pier. He took Rhonda's advice and figured that they might as well go out in style.

They arrived in Florida the next morning. Kile had taken them there at flank speed. It was a long day, but not over yet. First they had to deposit Ular II at the loading site for the super space shuttle, and pick up Raval. Next, check into a hotel. Once there they could refresh themselves, and make final plans for their trip to the station and their taking over the *Andromeda*. Later that evening Serik made a phone call to his friend, Dave, on the *New Hope* to have him meet them in the landing bay. This was the first time for Rhonda and Hellena to go openly among the surface dwellers.

Since they had two days to wait before the super shuttle's departure, Serik took everyone to a shopping mall where they soon purchased new "outsider" style clothing; next stop, a restaurant for brunch. The food was unusual to them, but Serik helped them along with their selections. This was indeed an adventure. Rhonda and Hellena were enjoying themselves very much. Later Serik took them to a cinema theater to watch one of the latest movies. The outside world seemed very strange to his companions. Rhonda remarked, "This city is extremely noisy."

Hellena added, "And it smells."

Serik remembered a spot where women scented themselves with oils. He took the two there, and the sales clerk showed them some of her most expensive merchandise. "Buy this one for me—will you?" asked Hellena cooing and batting her beautiful blue eyes at him. Both girls hardly looked a day over twenty-one. Serik gave in and bought it—this time with money he had exchanged for some of the gold coins he was given for expenses.

Time passed and soon the day was done. That night Serik called the space station once more. This time he talked with Angelica, his friend that worked in the programming department. He asked her to please meet him in the landing bay when he arrived. He only told her that it was of grave importance, and not to mention this phone call to anyone.

The next day the group went to Cape Kennedy. The project manager was there to greet them. "Your crate marked apparatus has been loaded into the shuttle's cargo bay. I didn't know what you wanted done with that small one, so I waited to load it until I got the word from you."

"Very good," remarked Serik. In a superior tone he inquired, "Is everything set for tomorrow's liftoff?"

The project manager replied, "Yes, but I had to hold back the space station's new solar mirror to make room for your apparatus."

"How is the weight limit holding out?" asked Serik.

"We're nearly to capacity, but we have a safe margin built in. I'm sure you are aware of that."

"Good, then there is room for three more passengers," remarked Serik.

"Th-three more passengers? I don't understand. I wasn't informed about three more passengers." Turning toward his office he continued, "I'll have to call and get clearances and verification."

But before he could make another move or say another word, Raval lowered his head slightly and closed his eyes. Serik soon followed suit, and as their minds met inside the project manager's, he turned around and said, "I guess it will be alright. After all, the head office did make exception and reschedule the cargo load out so you could take that apparatus along. They did say to help you out, and after all, I can sign the clearances myself."

Very good, came a soothing voice from within the manager's mind. "My assistants will need passes and flight suits issued to them. Can you arrange that now?" asked Serik vocally.

"Yeah—sure, follow me," and the project manager led them to his office. He had his secretary arrange for the passes right on the spot, and then he had her write out a voucher for the group to take to clothing issue for their flight suits. While the group was in his office, the project manager also made sleeping arrangements for them for the night. Tomorrow was the big day, launch and rendezvous with the space station, *New Hope.*

Before retiring for the night, Serik went to the cargo bay and communicated with Ular II about the past two day's events and what to expect the following day.

The next day was a busy one as the ground crew made final preparations for the flight. The cargo bay was loaded and secured. The super shuttle was lifted by the Cape's big crane and strapped into place alongside the booster rockets. Then the whole rocket assembly was slowly moved into place along the quarter mile track and fitted into the launch tower. Next, the liquid fuel was pumped into the quad rocket engine assemblies. When this phase was complete, the crew and passengers of the super space shuttle *Orion* were allowed to board. Counting the ship's crew and the three new passengers, the shuttle's manifest now logged a total of eleven persons. The countdown went as scheduled and the liftoff was uneventful. A quick trip, and two hours later they were docking in the landing bay. The landing bay was located in the center section where zero to low gravity was maintained. With a temporary storeroom nearby it made unloading the cargo bay much easier. Even the huge container marked apparatus was no problem for the shuttle's mechanical limb.

Angelica Adams and Dave Everett were waiting just outside the landing bay as they had promised Serik they would. After the group made their way through the air lock, Serik escorted them to the waiting room. He quickly introduced each member of his group. Gesturing to the two technicians, Serik said, "Angelica, Dave, I would like you to meet my Atlantian friends Hellena, Rhonda, and Raval." Angelica and Dave acknowledged them and offered a handshake.

"What is so important Serik that you called Angelica and me, and had us meet you here?" Dave inquired.

"Before I answer that question we have to find someplace more private," replied Serik, and led them out of the waiting room, down a corridor, turned left at the first junction past three doors to the right and into the fourth room marked life science office. Closing the door behind them and locking it, Serik gestured for everyone to sit down before he continued his explanation.

"I-ah-we need your help. What I am about to tell you cannot leave this room. Do you understand?" Both Angelica and Dave nodded their heads in affirmative. "Good—then what I am going to tell you is first going to shock you, and then you may disbelieve me. I assure you that what I am about to say is factual and unquestionably true. First, you know I am from Atlantis. As far as you care that is only some spot on a map, but what you probably don't know are the events that led to its raising.

"On our island, many of the sciences were pursued, one being bioengineering. Another science, what you might call occult, took everyday happenings and signs to help predict the future. Your kind has been using technology to try to forecast the weather. This is very similar, only more natural. We call this group of scientists soothsayers. Before I was conceived, the soothsayers predicted a massive earthquake in the vicinity of our island at the bottom of the ocean. Our city was destined for destruction unless something could be done. It was determined that by drilling a hole into the fault line farther down from the city, the pressure could be relieved and the earthquake averted. When doing so, the work force accidentally awakened the dormant volcano. When it erupted it hurtled our island to the surface where it remains today."

"So what is so secretive or urgent about that?" remarked Dave with sarcasm.

"Those same soothsayers have predicted the end of the world."

"Oh, come on. People have been predicting the end of the world since the beginning of time," interrupted Dave.

"But those people weren't Atlantian soothsayers! How can I convince you that our sciences have been long superior to yours for over a millennia?" Serik thought, and then asked, "How long can a man hold his breath? Three minutes? Four minutes? Ten minutes?"

"About five minutes has been the longest recorded time," remarked Dave with flippant indignation.

"Good. Check your watches and watch me very closely," instructed Serik.

He took a deep breath and held it. One minute passed, then two, then five, ten and at fifteen minutes Serik exhaled. Angelica and Dave were stunned. No one could do that. "How did you do it?" asked Angelica.

"Here look. You might as well know everything. We can't afford to have any secrets now between us," remarked Serik as he removed the flight jump suit then raised his shirt to reveal three folds of skin.

"What's that?" asked Angelica, unable to remove her eyes from his chest.

"Those are my gills," Serik flatly told her. "You see I can use them to breathe underwater and for short periods of time on the surface."

"So that's how you held your breath so long. You were breathing from your gills," stated Angelica.

"Correct, and as I was saying, our science is very advanced, so when I tell you the earth is going to self-destruct soon, I mean it," retorted Serik.

"Oh!" Angelica gasped, realizing that what he was telling them must be true. "But how?"

"A massive earthquake along the San Andreas fault will cause California to shift. When this happens the world is going to split apart. The California fault is the keystone to the world," Serik explained.

"When?" asked Angelica solemnly.

"The time frame has been predicted to be between one week and five more months," answered Serik.

Angelica then thought of the Atlantian's cure for their problem, and asked, "Why can't a hole be drilled along the fault to remove the pressure like your people did for your island?"

"No. That was the first idea explored. I'm afraid there is nothing that can be done to prevent this catastrophe," explained Serik.

"Why don't you warn the nations of the world, so they could prepare?" Dave accused.

"Prepare how? Even with your technology you couldn't build spaceships fast enough. Besides, can't you imagine the panic that information would cause?" asked Serik

"I see. I guess you are right." Pausing he continued, "but what does all this have to do with us?"

"The *Andromeda* is getting its final check-out this week. Next week it is scheduled for a test flight. Before the test flight we will need your help to get my apparatus onboard the ark and placed in one of its storerooms. Arrangements have been made to have the ark filled to capacity with food, supplies, spare parts, and fuel. Theoretically we need a more realistic test, but these arrangements have been made for us, all of us, if you are willing to help. The evening before the scheduled test flight we are going to steal the ark and fly it to a small planet near Alpha Centauri. We could use your expertise in computer programming and maintenance, and your expertise in propulsion. These talents are vital for a successful flight. We also need two surface dwellers to balance out the genetics to help us repopulate this planet," explained Serik.

"Repopulate?" asked Angelica, "Like Adam and Eve—to be the first people on this planet?"

"That's right," answered Serik. Then with a nod from Raval he continued to explain. "There is something else you might as well know. Some of us Atlantians can read minds. I am one of them."

"You're kidding! That's just a lot of fantasy—isn't it?" remarked Angelica.

Look at my lips and you tell me, Serik projected, *I can tell what you are thinking now, and if I try, I can learn what you know as if your knowledge and thoughts were mine. Not only that, but as you can see I can project my thoughts to you as easy as speaking to you.*

Amazing! came the pair's thoughts in unison, then Dave asked, "Who will fly the ark, and who will navigate?"

Still projecting, Serik continued, *Raval will fly the ark, and Ular*...as he projected an image of Ular's massive brain...*will navigate.*

"What, what was—I mean, who is Ular?" asked Angelica.

Raval projected his thoughts in answer. He also explained that if they didn't want to join them in this quest that Serik and himself could erase all memory of this conversation from their minds and, if necessary, absorb the required information that the two possessed in order for the group to complete their mission.

Before giving their reply, Angelica asked, "Can you place a thought into a person's mind without them knowing it, and have it time delayed to emerge sometime later after a key situation or happening occurs, as a control, to release that thought—sort of a post hypnotic suggestion?"

Raval and Serik conferred for a moment then Serik replied, "Yes, that can be done, but why do you want to know?"

Angelica looked at Dave. He didn't know what she was leading up to, but he instinctively trusted her and nodded to her reassuringly. "We'll go with you, but first you have to do something for us," Angelica offered.

"What is that?" asked Raval.

"I can program the onboard computer to the real-time clock, that two hours after our liftoff it will run the subroutine I shall put in its memory banks which will cause this station to leave geosynchronous orbit with the earth and head out into space beyond the moon. I can also program instructions on how to set it in a course for the space station to follow. That should keep the people on the station safe from this disaster you say is coming, and perhaps more than us six will be able to survive this event," explained Angelica.

"What good would that do?" asked Rhonda.

"It would save about two thousand more lives!" Angelica answered. "During the initial confusion of the station's departure from orbit there would be about twenty minutes to an hour before they could figure out a way to correct what I program into the computer."

She paused to check the other's understanding of what she was getting at. "That is where I need you. I need you to program into the station's director the realization that the earth is going to be destroyed, that there is nothing they can do to prevent it or help out, and that the guiding of the station out of orbit was planned, so that those aboard could possibly escape the earth's fate. I want him to understand that, and impress upon him not to take control away from the computer and return to geosynchronous orbit over the earth. He knows that the station is self-sustaining; thanks to the Atlantian influence," she chuckled.

"How long would it take you to write that program?" asked Serik.

"About two days," she answered.

"That is all the time we can give you." Angelica gave him a big hug. Then Serik turned to Dave. "We will need your help to get my apparatus onboard the ark, and any spare parts you think we may need." Turning his attention back to Angelica, he added, "Give me a list of anything you think we will need as well."

During the next two days Dave helped the Atlantians prepare the *Andromeda* for the longer journey. He helped them break into storerooms and remove valuable parts that were utilized in the ark. They even managed to fill the list Angelica had provided. A couple of extra space suits were liberated, and finally the task of moving the submersible into place.

The size alone made the task difficult. Fortunately the central non-gravity tunnel that passed through the axis of the station was wide enough to accommodate the large crate. As Raval, Dave and Serik pushed the container up to the ark's landing bay, Dave asked, "What's in this thing anyway?"

Raval bluntly answered, "A submersible."

"A what?"

"A submersible," Raval repeated and further explained, "The planet we are going to is much like earth. It may be covered with water. We will need some way to get around and explore for land, or to get us from one land mass to another."

"Oh, sorry I asked," Dave snidely remarked.

A day later an armed guard was posted outside the air locks that led to the *Andromeda*. Final systems check-out was complete, and station security didn't want to take any chances on anything happening to it prior to its maiden voyage. Angelica had programmed the computer. All that remained for them to do was to instill the thoughts and control trigger into the director's mind.

Serik brought Raval to the director's office door. On the door was printed ERIC WALKER, SYSTEMS PROJECT DIRECTOR. Serik knocked. "Come in," came a call from inside. When they stepped into the room, a tall, youthful, gray haired man, sporting a Vandyke, stood up from his desk to greet them. It was Eric Walker. His gray hair camouflaged the fact that he was one of the youngest members on the management team, only thirty-eight years old. He brought up his hand in a friendly gesture, "Good morning, what can I do for you?" It was his positive attitude that people liked most about him.

"I just brought my colleague in to introduce him," remarked Serik.

With a wide smile, hard to find on a Monday morning, Eric said, "Welcome. I'm in charge of this whole operation from here. My job is mainly to shuffle paperwork around, but if-ah-I-ah-I-ah-can help you-ah-I will..."

"That's OK. We mainly just came by to say hello," said Serik. "Thanks anyway," and then the two departed.

"That should take care of when the station leaves orbit. We had better meet with the others in my stateroom," Serik declared.

Once inside his stateroom he turned to Angelica and said, "We've done what we promised you. The thought has been implanted. Now I want everyone to go and get some rest because at five-thirty I'm going to wake all of you, and at six we're going to take over the ark and depart."

"Good," said Angelica. "I'll set the timer on my program for eight, and then go and get some rest myself. See you in the morning." She waved and departed down the corridor toward the main computer complex.

At 5:30 a.m. Serik started waking everyone and reminded them to be very quiet. By 6:00 the group was making its way down the corridor that led to the ark. Each member was carrying a bag with extra clothes in them. Before they reached the first junction in the corridor, Serik turned to face the others and projected into their minds, *Be very quiet. We don't want to be noticed. Dave, once we're inside I want you to start the engines. Angelica, I want you to open the outer bay door. Raval, after she opens the bay door I want you to damage the controller so that no one will be able to close it right away. After that, go to the control room and maneuver us out away from the space station.* Pausing he asked silently, *Any questions?*

Each member shook their head no.

The group rounded the bend to the left and followed that portion of the corridor to the next junction. Dave smiled grimly. So far so good. No one had spotted them. He wondered what they'd do if someone did. Probably act as if they were going to the exercise room. He wondered what Serik planned to do with that armed guard, oh well, surely he had some plan. He'd planned everything else out.

Keeping alert, Serik led the group to the junction that took them to the corridor to the *Andromeda*. One could feel the tension mount. So close, yet so far away. Serik stopped them and handed Raval his bag. Projecting to him, he instructed, *Wait here. I'll take care of the guard; then you bring the others in quickly!*

Raval gave him a singular affirmative nod and then Serik walked around the corridor. As he did so the guard quickly went from parade rest to port arms challenging his approach. Serik slowly advanced. The guard proceeded to aim his weapon at Serik and loudly and distinctly ordered, "Halt! Identify yourself."

Serik was in no mood to fool around. When he saw the guard raise his weapon, he levitated the guard off the floor and slammed him into the wall with such force as to render him unconscious. Serik mentally called to Raval to bring the others.

The group quickly took their positions. Angelica opened the outer bay door. As she did so it set off a security alarm. Inside the bay a series of red lights in the corners of the room began to flash. The alarm brought forth a multitude of people into the landing bay corridor. Serik noticed their approach and quickly conceived a wall of force to prevent their advance. One of the technicians was the first to arrive. He ran full tilt into Serik's shield and fell back on his butt, stunned. Before another person could run into it, the technician shouted, "Watch out, there's something in the way."

The next man to enter the corridor put his hands out in front of him and walked forward until he felt the invisible wall of force. He was both startled and amazed as he felt this resistant pressure. The attention of the crowd was now drawn to the invisible wall.

As all this was going on, Raval maneuvered the *Andromeda* out of the landing bay, turned on the main thrusters, and shot off into space. The group back at the station barely noticed the craft's departure until suddenly several of the pushing crowd fell onto the floor when Serik released the wall.

Angelica walked over to Serik and remarked, "I didn't know you could do that."

Serik replied, "Just goes to show what a little imagination can do," as he thought to himself, *I wasn't sure I could do that either.* Serik then went down into the cargo bay and emerged with Ular II. He carried Ular up to the control room and fastened his pillar onto the floor near the navigational control section. Proudly he announced to Angelica and Dave, "This is Ular, our navigator."

"Are you sure he can navigate? How can he read the charts or see any of the directional equipment?" asked Angelica in dismay.

"Come here and touch the sphere."

As she did so she noticed how cool and smooth it felt. Then she thought she sensed a twitch in her fingertips, and jerked her hands away. "Relax," Serik cooed. "Relax and open your mind." She placed her hands back on the cool, blue sphere while Serik said reassuringly, "Here, I'll help you," placing his hands over her own.

In silence she waited—then in her mind the gentle voice of an old man said, *Hello, I am Ular. You must be Angelica. Please do not fear me. You see, I need you as much as you need me. I live more each time someone communicates with me. I feel your feelings, and see with your eyes. I know your most private thoughts. I do not judge. I guide. Either through life or through space, it matters little to me. I am your friend.*

Excitedly she shouted, "I heard him! I heard him!"

"Heard what?" asked Dave.

"I heard Ular. He's great! It's—it's like talking with your father. Getting his advice, and consolation," she answered, and then blushed at her outburst.

Serik said with pride, "You are the first surface dweller to ever communicate with Ular."

"Can I do it again?" she asked enthusiastically.

"Please do. Ular needs a friend," replied Serik.

The space station was quick to report the ark as being stolen. Radio telescopes scanned the heavens for it, but with no luck. The news media on earth was quick to report the incident. Everywhere speculation and accusations sprang up. Many thought it was the Russians. Others thought it was the work of one of the numerous Middle East terrorist groups.

On Atlantis, Atar had his own technicians listen for any such news and when it finally came he and the council knew Serik's mission was underway. Atar ordered a celebration. No one knew why, but everyone was happy.

Two hours later the *New Hope* lurched out of orbit, and again a panic in space. "What's next?" yelled a frustrated technician.

Eric Walker became aware of the grievous truth—the fate of the world's demise and their own fate. He hastily arranged for his intercom to be patched into all levels of the station. "Attention! Please quiet down and give me your attention!" he paused to give everyone a chance to quiet down and himself a moment to gather his thoughts. "There is no cause for alarm. I have just been informed that the release into free space was deliberate. It appears that there is a problem on earth, and that they request that we make our way to the moon and await further instructions." Thinking quickly, he continued, "Your next of kin will be notified of our actions, and reports made of our safety. Due to the nature of this emergency, all communications will be limited and directed through this office. We need to make time available for official communications. In the meantime work will go on as usual." *Whew*, he thought, *I hope that announcement will calm them down.* He then switched off his inter-satellite intercom, and buzzed for his secretary. When she responded he said, "Get me communications!"

Rhonda gave Angelica and Dave an injection, and said to them, "This will improve your immune system and increase your longevity. However, you may need booster shots in about ten years." Rhonda thought to herself, *We finally got rid of that passing out side effect.*

"Where exactly are we going?" asked Dave.

"Come here, all of you," instructed Serik, standing by the blue sphere containing Ular. "Place your hands on the sphere. Form a large circle with your hands. Relax," Serik began in a calm, reassuring manner, "Relax. Open your minds and Ular will explain."

In their minds the universe began to open up to them. Galaxies passed by in a blur of light until, near a small star, an image of a planet began to become sharper. It was as if they were flying in from space and approaching the planet in order to make a landing. Through the cloud cover, vast land masses started to take shape and become clear. Each huge mass was surrounded by water. Huge continents were taking shape, but none of them resembled anything like that of earth. As these images appeared in their minds, each could not help but to be awe-struck. The image paused over a green, forest covered continent, then again, as if they were gently gliding closer to the land they started to make out trees, and strange-colored birds flying in the sky. The birds didn't resemble any on earth. The trees were full of autumn color. Soon they had glided down until it was as if they had made contact with the ground. Then within their minds, amongst these images, a kindly old man's voice spoke, *Behold that which you seek. Behold wonder and rejoice for this is your new home. Your new Atlantis—Atlantis II.*

- THE END -

CPSIA information can be obtained at www.ICGtesting.com
Printed in the USA
LVOW12s1403221113

362430LV00001B/60/P